Dave

Read & enjoy.

Look out for the

generated ghost.

Unc. Larry

As Life Moves On

Larry Webb

2

To Kay

My love, my best friend, my wife

As Life Moves On

Chapter 1

Tied to our chairs, we watched Bruno slowly meander over to the work bench and snatch that large butcher knife sticking out of its top. He cackled this God awful, sick, eerie laugh under his breath, and then he started singing some hideous song I'd never heard before. It terrified me. He wasn't just trying to scare us, he actually planned to slit our throats and throw us into that barrel of acid. He roughly grabbed the front of my shirt with his left hand while clutching the knife in his right. The sneer on his face... I screamed!

...

I woke up wringing wet with cold, clammy sweat drenching my entire body. I've had other strange psychic like visions during the day about Marty's stepdad, Bruno Bashore, ever since the

4

judge sent that lunatic to the nut house for killing Marty's mom. I'm sure they're somehow related to the fact that he threatened to kill both of us when the officers led him out of the courthouse after his trial. However, this is the first time I've dreamed the vision. I don't suppose that Scott's ghost showing up last night just before I went to sleep telling me that Bruno had escaped would have anything to do with the dream I just had either, would it? Yeah, right! Thanks, Scott!

Fortunately, my screaming didn't wake up the Rents. Maybe it only happened in my dream. I hope so. They don't know about my psychic like visions, or, in this case, nightmares about that weirdo. Oh well, I can't dwell on that. I've got to get my butt out of bed. It's Monday morning, and I need to get ready for school. Only a couple of weeks left before vacation—can't wait!

After breakfast I met up with Marty in the driveway that runs between our houses, and we headed out. I didn't say anything to him about the dream. He still suffers from the actions of his deranged stepdad so he doesn't need to hear about my problems. We pulled into the student parking lot to quite a surprise. Cop cars were parked all over the place including the one driven by our old buddy Detective Sergeant Sean O'Connor. When we walked up to the gym door, where we normally entered the school, an officer stood there directing foot traffic away from the locker room.

"What's going on?" I asked trying to see around him.

"Have to use one of the other doors this morning, boys. Nobody's allowed in here until the area gets cleared by the investigating officers," he told us.

"So what happened?" I asked again wondering why they were there and if he would actually tell us. Marty didn't say anything, but he tried to gawk through the door to see if he could see anything going on. He couldn't. That fat cop blocked our view.

"Just some vandalism over the weekend. Can't say that much about it. You'll hear all the details as soon as you get in the building," he replied laughing. He knew how fast gossip flew inside a high school. "You'll just have to use one of the other doors this morning."

Marty and I bitched all the way to the front door. "Typical cop!" Marty grumbled. "Nothing like blowing us off. Jerk!"

"I know," I complained. "No reason he couldn't tell us. It's not like it would hurt anything."

"Yeah, I know. Too bad O'Connor isn't at the door. He'd tell us," Marty answered.

"We saw his car out back so he's gotta be inside someplace checking out whatever happened," I said. "That's better yet. We'll get all the inside dirt that way," I laughed as we made our way around the building to the front door.

Looked like they'd herded the entire school into the commons area just inside the door to wait for whatever was going on to clear up. Kids and teachers alike all clustered themselves around into little groups—some at the lunch tables, and some just standing around. Conversations and speculation ran rampant. However, nobody seemed to have a real good handle on what had happened. If the teachers did, they weren't telling us.

Maybe fifteen minutes after the first hour bell rang, Mr. Bishop, the principal, came out and shouted at us, "Everyone go ahead and head to first hour class now."

Naturally, he didn't give us any details either—just go to class and clear the halls. The teachers all started shooing us towards the hallways like we were a herd of cattle or something. As Marty and I started walking towards our wing, the principal flagged us down.

"Jeremy, Marty, I'd like a word with you. Would you come with me, please?" he asked as he turned around and headed for his office. He didn't even look back to see if we followed.

"Have a seat, guys," he said pointing to a couple of chairs. "I need to get this note to the secretary before she reads the morning announcements. Be right back."

"What the hell does he want?" I asked Marty under my breath as soon as he walked out of the door.

7

"Beats me! Have to admit, though, it makes me a bit on the nervous side. It's not like we're regular guests to the inner sanctum."

Not more than a minute or two later Mr. Bishop returned, sat down, folded his hands, and just looked at us for a few seconds before saying anything. "Good morning, boys. I have something to ask you, and I'd like a straight forward answer. I think I know what you're going to say, but I need to ask you anyway. Did either one of you come back to the school over the weekend?"

"No! I spent the whole weekend at home working on that huge English project for Mr. Andrews," I said wondering why he'd singled us out when there were 600 or so other kids in the school. Obviously, whatever had happened had something to do with all the cops being in the gym.

"Mrs. Mercer had to work overtime at the hospital so I stayed at her house almost all weekend having absolutely no life of my own. Between babysitting for Bobby, Emily, and working on the project, I did nothing else. Period! So why are you asking us about our weekends?" Marty asked in a tone hinting of just a little bit of a chip on the shoulder. That didn't sound like him at all.

"Somebody broke in and vandalized the gym over the weekend," he answered ignoring Marty's obvious irritation. "I'm sure that the police will want to talk to you this morning so I might as well tell you what I know. Someone took a knife or something sharp and carved up all three wrestling mats and completely destroyed the main one. Then they spray painted an ominous note on the side of the mat stating, 'Marty and Jeremy— you gonna die!'"

"Bruno!" Marty and I both gasped at the same time as we looked at each other. It had to be him. Who else?

"So, who've you guys been fighting with that'd be mad enough to trash the mats and write a stupid threatening note on the thing for evidence," Mr. Bishop asked ignoring our Bruno declarations. "Sounds to me like somebody either really hates the two of you, or somebody's got a pretty warped sense of humor. Or, of course, it could be just plain old malicious destruction, and they put your names on the mat to throw everybody off. Any ideas?"

"It sounds like something Bruno, my so-called step dad, would do except for the fact that he's in the state mental hospital. We all know he's crazier than a loon; but, he shouldn't be out yet. He's only been in there two months," Marty said.

"I seriously doubt that your dad or any other adult would ever do anything like that even if he did suffer from mental issues. The whole thing looks too much like kid's work," he said. "Besides, like you said, there's no way Mr. Bashore could have been released all ready. Let's face it, Marty; he did murder your mother. He's not going anywhere for a long, long time if ever. So let's brainstorm here a little. Have you two been bullying or picking on anybody lately? Is there anyone out there that you know is mad at you?"

"No, we haven't done a thing like that. We don't bully people. I still think it had to be Bruno. You just don't know him like I do," Marty said very softly as he withdrew into his own little world no longer showing any if that little flash of anger he'd showed previously, just sadness.

Just the mention of Bruno cranked up the depression in Marty, and he would look and sound so sad. I always tried very hard not to even mention the creep if I could help it. Besides, he considered Jim Dad and Mom Sara as his parents now anyway so why bother?

"Oh well! I did want to kind of warn you about what happened since it does sound like somebody might be trying to get you into trouble or scare you, one of the two. Why don't you go on to class and not say anything to anyone about the threat? I'm sure that the news will spread fast enough without your help. The police will probably talk to you when they finish down in the gym so stay in class and don't be sneaking out of school or anything," he said smiling only half picking on us.

He knew we wouldn't do that now, especially with all the police and excitement at school. No way did we want to miss anything. However, I suppose he thought he needed to get his point across and make sure we stayed available. It wouldn't look too cool if the police decided to talk to us, and we were at the soda shop down on the avenue or at the food court in the mall. It wouldn't be the first time we'd done it during school hours, but today wouldn't be one of them.

As soon as we walked out the door, I turned to Marty and said, "Before we go to class, we need to talk. Let's find an empty room."

"Ok, the computer lab behind the library is usually empty first hour. Let's check it out."

We were in luck. Nobody was in there, and the lights were out so we slipped in and went to the back of the room, sat down, and turned on a couple of the computers to make it look like we were working in case anyone came in.

"Marty, what I'm gonna tell you sounds really freaky and you're probably gonna think I'm nuts."

"So, try me. Probably won't think you're any freakier than normal," Marty grinned.

"A week after Scott was killed I went to the cemetery for the first time, and saw him and his dog Mooshy sitting on his burial mound."

"Whoa!" Marty exclaimed. "How did that happen? What do you mean?"

"I can see and talk to Scott and Mooshy's ghosts."

"Cool! Tell me all about it," Marty said wide eyed and engrossed.

"I can't tell you everything, at least not all at once. And for God's sake, Marty, promise me you'll keep everything I tell you a secret? I've never told anyone else except for a couple of people who also can see things. My parents don't even know."

"No problem on this end. After all you've done to help me, there's no way I'd screw you up. So, what's going on? Why are you telling me now?"

"Bruno escaped yesterday. Scott slipped in and told me within a couple hours or so after it happened. Typically, when he needs to get me information or contact me about something, he does it at night after I go to bed. He and Mooshy just show up," I told him.

"No kidding?" Marty exclaimed.

"Yeah, I'm sorry I didn't tell you about it earlier. I just wanted to wait until the police or the media said something. Then with the mat damage and the threat, I had to tell you." What I didn't do was tell him about the dream that woke me up. I had to hold off on that for the time being.

"Man! That just about blows my mind. You said there are a couple of other people who can see Scott. Anyone I know?"

"You're sworn to secrecy, right?"

"Promise!"

"Nobody else knows about Scott and me except for Bobby and Sergeant O'Connor."

"Bobby? The kid I babysit for?"

"Yes. He's fully sensitive to Scott's spirit. He talks to him out at the cemetery when his mom goes to visit his dad's grave. But he knows it's a big secret so they communicate telepathically all the time just like Scott and I do. It's happened a couple of other times too like at the mall and at his house."

"He's never mentioned anything at all," Marty said.

"I know. He's really smart and knows that he has to keep the whole thing hush-hush. Scott convinced him that it's a big secret, and that they don't want to make his mom or anyone else feel bad so they can't tell anyone. That's why he hasn't said anything."

"What about O'Connor?"

"He knows all about Scott but can't see or hear him. He has a slight sensitivity to the spirit world so the phenomenon really intrigues him. After meeting him sometime back when Scott and I were trying to figure out what had happened with his accident, we've talked fairly regularly."

"What kind of stuff does he want to talk about?" Marty asked.

"He acts like he's half jealous of my sensitivity and his lack of," I laughed. "He's always asking about what he can do to make himself more accessible to his own powers. He wants to be able to see and talk to Scott so bad he can practically taste it. I've no clue what to tell him other than to relax and not fight it like Grandma told me to do after she died."

"Your grandmother talked to you after she died?"

"Yeah, I spoke to her ghost a few days after she died, and she also sent me a message through Scott later on."

"Awesome! Anyone else?"

"My mom has something going on too, but neither one of us has ever mentioned it to the other. My sensitivity comes down from her side of the family."

"How do you know?"

"That's what Grandma told me after she died. Her family thinks their sensitivities started wearing out with each new generation. Mom has a very slight sensitivity. According to Grandma, sometimes Mom will get a flash of something, and then she tries to block it out. Grandpa thought that Mom and Grandma had emotional issues and urged both of them to fight off the flashes of intuition when they had them. I think that's why she's never mentioned it to me. I don't even know if Dad knows. Anyway, apparently I'm the exception to the rule. Since I've never tried to block the visions, the sensitivity, or whatever you call it, seems to be growing stronger—maybe because of my relationship with Scott? Who knows?"

"So do you think Bruno did the mat stuff? Sure sounds like a possibility," Marty asked looking off into space again.

"I really don't know. However, if anyone says anything about it, we've got to play dumb.

By the time we made it to English class third hour, the room literally buzzed. Mr. Andrews had disappeared someplace. Not real surprising. As wrestling coach, he practically considered the mats and equipment his own private property. It turned into a free hour for us because no sub showed up either. By then everyone knew about the threat written on the mat so a crowd gathered around our table wanting all the details. At that point we really didn't know anymore than they did. We sure weren't going to tell anyone what we suspected.

15

We sat there talking to our friends for maybe fifteen minutes when a girl from the office showed up at the door with a note from the principal telling Marty and me that he wanted us in the conference room. I'm sure that gave the class something to really chatter about after we left. They probably figured we were suspects or something.

"Now what?" Marty grumbled as we headed down the hall.

"Has to be more about those darn mats. Probably the cops want to grill us now," I said hoping it would be Sean O'Connor doing the inquisition.

"Wonder if they found out anything," he said. "Just don't understand why anyone other than Bruno would do something like that. It had to be him. But, why? Is he just trying to scare us?"

"Yeah, I know what you're saying especially since he did escape last night. Remember, we gotta play dumb on that one. Anyway, I can't imagine why he'd come back here though when all the cops in town know him. If it was me, I'd head out for parts unknown as fast as possible," I said trying to downplay the possibility of it being Bruno even though I thought that it probably was. If that little mess in the gym was an attempt to scare us, it worked.

When we showed up at the office, the secretary told us to head right straight back to the conference room. Much to our surprise Mom and Mom Sara, both sat there along with Sergeant O'Connor, the principal, and a couple other people we didn't know. During the introductions we learned that one was a detective and the other was from the state hospital for the criminally insane.

Anytime Detective Sergeant Sean O'Connor had ever talked to me about official police business—like after Scott's death, I called him Officer O'Connor. When he tried to pump me about my sensitivity to Scott's ghost, he wanted me to call him Sean. This time we kept everything pretty formal.

As soon as Marty and I sat down after the introductions, O'Connor looked around at everyone and started speaking, "I asked that a parent or guardian for both boys attend this meeting because of the nature of the situation. I think that by now everyone knows about the vandalism over the weekend to the wrestling mats and the graffiti that someone painted on one of them which constituted a threat on Marty and Jeremy's lives. What you don't know is that Mr. Bashore escaped from the state mental hospital last night. From what they've been able to determine at the hospital, he hid in the bottom of a laundry cart that was full of sheets."

17

Both moms gasped as Marty and I faked surprise as well. "How'd it happen?" Marty asked really wanting to know since we didn't know how he'd managed to do it.

"They transport filled laundry carts out of the facility every Sunday evening to an offsite laundry where they wash the bedding on Monday and then return it later in the day. Normally they search the carts very carefully. In fact the driver and one of the guards both claimed that they'd checked the carts. However, after the search, they left them unattended for maybe two or three minutes when the driver made a quick trip to the men's room before he headed out.

"Now, that doesn't guarantee that Mr. Bashore had anything to do with this, but we can't rule him out either. Anyone have any questions or anything to say before I continue?" O'Connor asked.

"My biggest concern's for the safety of the boys," Mom stated. "Has there been any sign that he's actually in the area?"

Mom Sara, Scott's mom and Marty's foster mom all rolled into one, nodded in agreement. "Do we need to take the boys out of school until the authorities capture him or what?"

"We don't really know where he is, but I don't think we need to be overly concerned about their well being," O'Connor said. "They should be fine here at school and at home. What I would like to see, though, just to be on the safe side, is that neither one of them goes anywhere alone at any time until this thing resolves itself. Marty, are you still babysitting every day after school?"

"Yes. Jeremy drives me to day care where I pick up Emily and Bobby, and then he drops me off at Bobby's house where I stay with the kids until Mrs. Mercer comes home from work. Then she gives Emily and me a ride home." Emily is Scott's baby sister who was born six months after he died.

"So, Jeremy, would you be willing to stay with Marty at the Mercer's after school until Bruno is recaptured?" O'Connor asked. "I don't want you home alone either. I'll call Mrs. Mercer before this meeting's over and make she's ok with the idea. She might not want to take any chances either by putting Bobby in any danger, even though I don't think that'd be the case."

"Sure! That's no big deal for me. I can always do my home work or help Marty with the kids if he needs it." I answered.

"Do you think either boy is in more danger than the other," Sara asked.

"I really don't know, to be perfectly honest with you. I just don't want either one of them anywhere alone right now until Mr. Bashore is either captured or we can confirm that he has left the area."

O'Connor made his call to Mrs. Mercer, and she agreed with the plan after Sean answered some of her questions and concerns apparently to her satisfaction. Everyone also settled on the fact that Marty and I would stick together like glue until the dads came home from work in the evening. That worked well with the two of us. We got along fine, and neither wanted to take the chance of running into Bashore while we were all alone. The guy was huge, scary, and crazy as a freaking banshee.

As we walked out of the conference room, Sean slipped up beside me and whispered, "Did you know about Bashore escaping last night before I told you?"

I just glanced at him and nodded slightly.

"I figured as much," he said as he ambled away. "We need to talk later."

Chapter 2

The rest of the day was hectic to say the least. Word spread like wild fire that the cops had dragged Marty and me into the conference room with our parents. Some actually thought the police probably suspected us of the vandalism. One person even had the balls to come right out and ask me if we did it. Needless to say, that jerk didn't hit the top of the chart for our "Friend of the Month" club. Most everyone just wanted to know what we knew—which really wasn't much.

The end of the day couldn't get there fast enough. When the final bell rang, Marty and I raced to our lockers, grabbed what we needed, and headed out. We planned to go grab the kids from daycare and head to Mercer's house after a little side trip to the food court at the mall. We figured we'd feel safer there with all the people around than we would being alone. We'd arrived at school later than usual that morning so we'd parked way out in back of the student parking lot. It took a little hike to get to the building from there. The parking lot was shaped like a giant L with that back section somewhat secluded and hidden from view from the school. Kids, who wanted that last cigarette before heading into the building, parked back there intentionally.

About fifty feet away from the car, Marty said under his breath, "Oh, oh!"

"What?" I asked picking up on the tone of his voice.

"Hold it! Look at your tires," he said stopping in his tracks.

I looked ahead at my car and saw what had made him gasp and skid to a halt. All four tires lay flat. "Oh, crap!" I said. "Now what're we going to do?"

"Better call O'Connor before we go anywhere near your car," Marty insisted. "Hell, it might be booby trapped or something. At this point, who knows?"

"Oh, come on! We don't have terrorists around here, but you might be right about calling just to be on the safe side. Besides, I don't want to get chewed out for not letting him know," I said digging my cell phone out of my pocket. I had Sergeant O'Connor on my speed dial under 'Sean.' I pushed the button and waited.

"Yeah, Jeremy, what's up?" he answered after checking his caller id.

"Marty and I are in the school parking about twenty feet from my car walking real slowly towards it trying to get a good look without going right up to it. From here it appears like maybe somebody flattened all four tires. Don't know if they slashed them or just let the air out. With everything that's going on, we didn't know if we should check out the car or not. Marty thinks it might be wired to blow up or something. I think maybe he watches CNN too much. I wanna go take a look. That ok?"

"No! Marty's right. Stay away from the car. Go back inside of the building and head to the main office right now and wait for me. Where's your car parked?"

"Way out in back of the L close to the tree line," I told him.

"I'm on my way. Go in and tell the principal what happened, and then call your parents and let them know. See if someone will come and pick the two of you up. Marty better call the day care and Mrs. Mercer. Other people might have to pick up the kids this afternoon. I'm not sure yet. All I know is I want you in the school office now!" and then he pushed the "End" key. Sergeant O'Connor tended to do that especially when he didn't want an argument.

We actually did what he said without complaining too badly and headed back to the building leaving the car flat on the ground. Mr. Bishop stood outside of his office door on patrol making him easy to find for a change. After school he might be anywhere. Not too predictable. Damn!

"Mr. Bishop," I said when we approached.

"What?" he asked with that principal styled 'Now what?' look on his face as he raised his eyebrows.

"Somebody flattened all the tires on my car. I've already called the police and the cop insisted that we wait in the main office."

"Actually, I'd feel more comfortable if you waited in my office. Go inside, close the door and lock it, and pull down the window and door shades so nobody can see you in there. I'm going to wander out into the parking lot and check for smokers. Where exactly did you park?"

"Way out in the back lot," I told him.

"Ok, you know, this really has to be some kind of a kid's prank—somebody just hassling you thinking it's funny. You know, just because Mr. Bashore escaped doesn't mean he's around here causing problems for you guys. I still think he's probably long gone."

Outwardly we agreed with him, but inside we knew better. Hiding inside his office wouldn't make it any easier either. I wanted to be out where I could run if I had to. Like I could out run a bullet or something if Bruno really wanted to get us!

While we sat in Mr. Bishop's office, we called the Rents, day care, and Mrs. Mercer. Mrs. Mercer said not to worry because she would pick up Bobby herself when she left work. Mom Sara said she would pick up Emily and that someone would come and get us. She wasn't sure but thought it would probably be Jim Dad. Good, at least we didn't have to worry about babysitting the kids. That really didn't appeal to me—especially right then. I had too many other things on my mind.

Wasn't too much later when Sean O'Connor walked in with Mr. Bishop, "Hi, guys. Everyone doing ok?"

"Yeah, sure!" We both answered lying through our teeth. We'd both been freaking out inside. I'll probably get ulcers.

"Good! Jeremy, let me have your keys. They slashed all four tires with a knife or something so I do want to check the car thoroughly inside and out to make sure it hasn't been messed with like Marty suggested. I'm sure everything is fine, but just in case, stay in here until I come back."

"Bummer! I said to Marty as soon as they left. "I never thought anyone would take you seriously about that possibility. This bull's getting serious."

25

"Just tell me that Bishop is right and that it's some kid that's doing all of this!" Marty said very visibly shook up.

"Has to be! No way would Bruno stay in this area," I tried to convince Marty not believing a word of it. "Probably one of those idiots who think we actually had something to do with the mats getting cut trying to 'show us!'"

Not a whole lot later both dads arrived on the scene. They rode together and walked out to check up on what the police were doing before coming in to find us. In the meantime, Marty and I barricaded ourselves in the principal's office bored out of our minds trying to convince ourselves that we were perfectly safe. Finally they all came back in to get us.

"Come on, guys. We're going home now," Dad said. "Sorry you missed all the excitement, but I called a wrecker and they've already towed your car."

"Hey! No fair! We didn't even get a chance to see it up close!" I complained. That sucked big time.

"That's okay. You'll get a chance to check out the four brand new tires that you'll have to ride on this winter. Glad we bought insurance for that thing."

Everyone acted a little on the paranoid side. So before we left, Sean suggested, "Why don't you pull all the shades and drapes on the main floor for both houses when it gets dark for a while so nobody passing by a window can look in."

"Yeah," I said quickly to O'Connor. "My bedroom sits at the back of the house on the main floor, and the thought of sleeping in bed with Bruno Bashore gawking at me through the window turns my stomach. I'll pull down my shades—probably should do it anyway, but I like to feel the breeze blowing in on me when I'm sleeping."

Mom came up with an even better idea when we got home. "Why don't you, at least for now, just move into the guest bedroom off the family room downstairs? That way nobody's going to be able to see you."

"I'll do it," I replied without any argument. "In fact, I'll do it right now! The whole idea of that nutcase being able to gawk at me through window gives me the creeps."

The body shop finally brought my car back on Wednesday, but it didn't really matter. I couldn't drive it to school anyway. Dad made me park it in the garage with the doors down and locked. "At least my car looks good," I told Marty. "Not only does it have four brand new shiny tires, they even washed it."

"Wonder how long it will be before things can get back to normal?" Marty asked as we checked it out through the garage window with everything all locked up and the keys in dad's pocket.

Mom took Marty and me to school in the morning, and we had to take the bus home in the afternoon. There would be no babysitting for Marty that week with either kid or trips to the mall food court for us after school. The moms put the little ones in full time daycare temporarily. The "No trips to the food court or anywhere else!" hurt the most. That one sucked big time. The Rents totally grounded us, and it wasn't even our fault—for a change.

"Jeremy, do you realize that our lives have turned us into a couple of paranoid nerds spending every afternoon together at home pacing the floor with the shades and drapes pulled wondering where the hell Bruno is and if he's watching us? Is he still planning on doing away with us? Has he left the state? And why haven't the police caught him yet?"

"I know. Freaky, isn't it? This can't go on forever. We'll both go nuts!" I tried to reassure him.

By the following week nobody had seen or heard of Bruno Bashore. No more vandalism or threats of any kind occurred so things started to quiet down a little.

School let out for the summer and we were really going nuts. So, one night when the six of us ate dinner together, I spoke for

Marty and me—we'd planned my little speech in advance, "It's more or less assumed now that Bruno's headed out for parts unknown. He's very recognizable, and all the cops know him and have been looking out for him. Yet nobody has spotted him. No way would he hang around town any longer than he had to. If this seclusion thing stretches on too much more, Marty and I will both end up basket cases. We've got to get our lives back to normal. It's like we're the ones being punished for something that Bruno did."

Seems like the Rents had been thinking pretty much along the same lines. After a lot of discussion among them, the day care, Mrs. Mercer, and even Marty and me—along with a phone call or two to Sean, everyone finally decided that we could gradually get our lives back to normal.

Marty would return to his babysitting duties like always. Nobody could see any reason why either Bobby or Emily should be in any danger so why not? For the first week I would stay there with him, surf the Internet, check my email, and play "Mad Demons" on Mrs. Mercer's computer. She was good enough to let me install it.

Absolutely nothing out-of-the-ordinary happened that next week so we started making our daily food court excursions to the mall, Then, it got to the point where I'd take Marty to the Mercers, hang out for a while, and then go home. Mrs. Mercer went back to driving Marty and Emily home after she came home from work, and everything pretty much went back to the way it had been before—with a few exceptions, of course.

Chapter 3

Eventually, the summer vacation passed and school loomed again just around the corner. Scottie died just over a year ago. A lot had happened. Fortunately nobody had seen or heard anything from or about Bruno Bashore for several months so the tension and pressure faded, and our lives gradually returned to normal. I moved my bedroom back upstairs, and even started leaving the shade up a little so the breeze could blow in on me. Marty babysat every day and hoarded his money. He wanted his own car so bad he could taste it.

Marty had never driven a car before Jim Dad took him out the first time.

"I really have no clue about what I'm doing," he told Jim Dad on that first trial run. Don't remember how I happened to be riding along in the back seat, but there I sat watching and remembering. Fortunately I had enough sense to keep my mouth shut. The whole thing scared him to death as it was without my adding my two cents worth—just a tad different from when Scott and I first drove.

"Just relax and pay attention to what I tell you," Jim Dad told him. "Everything will be fine."

"This is the first time I've ever sat behind the wheel when the motor was running. Bruno wouldn't let me drive or take driver's education. Said we couldn't afford it," Marty said wide eyed as he stared straight ahead with a death grip on the wheel.

Jim Dad had been right. Everything went fine. Fortunately, over time he managed to take driver's ed, get in all his hours, and pass his written and driving tests before his seventeenth birthday thanks to the two sets of rents. Mom Sara, Jim Dad, and my mom and dad took turns letting him drive. Finding the time was tough because he worked every day with the two kids, and then he had his "life of my own" to take care of. He'd been scouting some girl hot and heavy at the food court. Like everybody else, he burned the the candle at both ends and had very little actual down time.

To celebrate his birthday, the six of us went out to dinner Friday night at our favorite restaurant. He received cards from both sets of parents and the waiters and waitresses all sang a ghastly rendition of "Happy Birthday" that embarrassed him to death. We found it hilarious watching the crimson flash in his cheeks. I kept waiting for the old folks to do something special but nothing happened. Marty looked happy as a clam and smiled all during dinner. He hadn't had a birthday celebration of his own in years. He seemed more than satisfied by just going out to dinner and getting a couple of cards.

When we left, they pulled the same stunt on him that they had done to me on my seventeenth. We finished dinner, walked out to Jim and Sara's car, and then they stopped at the car parked beside it and handed him a set of keys and told him to try the door. Then they had him get in and try the ignition. Then both sets handed him a fifty dollar bill and told him "Happy Birthday!" again. Marty bawled like a baby. He never, ever expected anything like that. The four rents had gone together and bought him a car just like they'd done for me on my seventeenth a few months earlier.

Marty passed all kinds of sloppy wet hugs and tears around to everybody. Any passerby witnessing the scene would have thought something devastating had just happened. I even got a hug from him. About then Jim Dad spoke up. "Ok, you guys. It's time for the two of you to get out of here. Be home by midnight."

Not sure if Marty wanted me to tag along on his maiden voyage or not, I kind of stood back and waited. This was his day. When he had the seats and mirrors all adjusted and ready to go, he looked over at me and said, "Get in, Jeremy! I need a navigator."

Very funny! Everyone laughed at my expense. I'm terrible at directions and am the first to admit it. When I first started driving solo, they accused me of using my GPS unit to get back and forth from home to school. That, of course, only slightly exaggerated the truth.

Five hours and a half tank of gas later, we pulled into the driveway just a few minutes before midnight. Marty's mouth ran like a clapper on a duck's butt the entire time. All I had to do was answer, "Yeah, uh huh, yep."

"I've got to be dreaming. I can't believe what's happened today," he kept saying over and over every five minutes or so.

I've never seen anyone so happy and wound up about anything. I thought I'd been excited when I got my car—that was nothing compared to Marty. I've lived a good life for seventeen years with the exception of losing Scott. Marty has enjoyed a good life for the past five or six months. There's a big difference. I would take no bets on how much actual sleep he managed to get that night.

I did fine. The nice thing about Saturdays during the school year is being able to sleep in until at least nine am. That's much better than the six thirty alarm on weekdays when school is in session. In the summer and on weekends, if I'm not up and about by nine, The Rents start yelling at me. "You gonna sleep all day? Has rigor mortis set in? Are you physically attached to that

34

bottom sheet and mattress? Get your butt out of bed!" Just once it would be nice to have them just leave me alone. I'd love to sleep in until noon at least one time.

As it worked out, I lounged around all morning, ate breakfast, read the sports page, and did pretty much nothing in particular. About one I received a text message from Marty, "Food court – mall – I'll drive."

My, what a surprise! He wants to drive his car, I thought to myself. It took me about five minutes to get ready before I flew out the door. I'd been thinking that I might put my application in a couple of the fast-food joints there at the mall. I seriously considered that maybe the time had come where I should be a little more financially self sufficient. In other words, maybe I should get a job that would carry me over the winter months?

The economy still sucked, but I figured I should be able to find something if I worked at it hard enough. I really considered that I should quit mooching so much off of the old folks. During the spring and summer I worked at the golf course on the weekends for coach who supervised the place out there, but that didn't do much for my cash supply the rest of the year. Besides, summer was almost over and except for weekends, I'd be out of a job as soon as school started. Golf leagues would start winding down and the days would start getting a little shorter, and I wouldn't be needed as much.

Fortunately for our family, Dad's job had returned to normal. During the time when construction was way down, he only managed to put in half days at the architectural firm where he works. Our family finances sucked then and helping with Marty's car would not have been even remotely possible. With the new president and congress, the economy started to turn around so construction kicked in again. That meant he had gone back to work full time. Halleluiah for the family budget and my allowance! Maybe I didn't need to be in such a rush to get a job after all?

When we pulled into the mall parking lot, there appeared to be a lot of commotion going on. At least six police cars could be seen in the front parking lot including Sergeant Sean O'Connor's whose overhead lights were flashing. As we climbed out of the car and headed to the door, I looked at Marty and said, "Now what?"

Things had been so quiet in our little world the past few months it kind of upset me to see so many police cars all gathered in the same location.

"Somebody probably robbed one of the food court joints," Marty commented with a smirk on his face. "Nothing like gambling 20 years of your life in jail over a couple hundred bucks. Duh!"

"Nobody ever said that the typical crook is too smart," I answered. "Oh well, maybe we'll get a chance to say 'Hi' to O'Connor. Haven't seen him for a while."

36

He took me out to lunch earlier in the summer so he could actually talk to someone who understands his flashes of insight or whatever you want to call it when one sees the unexplainable. However, I don't think I'd seen him in the past six weeks or so.

Talk about surprises! When we reached the food court, there sat Mrs. Mercer at a table in tears. Sean O'Connor had his butt parked in the seat next to her patting her hand, trying to calm her down. I took a quick look around. Didn't see Bobby anywhere. Since Marty wasn't babysitting, he should have been with her.

Marty gave me a quick panicked look and bolted to their table. "Where's Bobby?" Marty demanded without even as much as a "Hi!" or "What's the matter?"

"I don't know. He's gone. We can't find him."

"What happened?" I asked.

"Bobby needed some new shoes. His old pair had gotten pretty scruffy looking. When we walked into the mall, he saw some kid walking along with lights on his that blinked on and off. Surprise! Surprise! That's what he wanted so I bought him a pair. He got all excited and jabbered away like always. I really didn't pay all that much attention to him. I just let him run around the store showing everyone in the place his shoes. When I went up to pay for them, I told him to sit in the chair until I finished. I just wanted to get them paid for so we could get out of there, and I

37

could keep my sanity. He can be a handful at times as you well know.

"He started yelling, 'I wanna show Marty and Jeremy my new shoes at the food court,' He just assumes you spend all your time there when you aren't with him.

"So I told him, 'Wait until I'm done here. We'll make sure that Marty and Jeremy see them. Just sit patiently for a couple more minutes.'

"So then he said something like, 'Gonna go show Marty and Jeremy now,' without it fully registering on me what he'd just said. My credit card hadn't processed immediately so I'd been paying attention to that. The girl said they'd been running slow all day.

"After the charge finally went through, it suddenly dawned on me what he really said. I wheeled around looking for him and he'd vanished."

Then Sergeant O'Connor started talking, "We kind of assume that he went off by himself looking for you two. How long have you been around? Did you see him anyplace?"

"No! We just walked in the door. Besides, if we'd seen him out wandering around by himself, we'd of grabbed him and gone to find Ginny," I said. The inference ticked me off just a little.

"Yeah, we sure wouldn't have just left him wandering around by himself for cripes sake," Marty snapped back at him.

"Lighten up, guys!" O'Connor said. "I didn't mean it the way it sounded. Of course you wouldn't have left him running around all by himself. Give me a little slack here. I'm just trying to put all the pieces together in my head and figure out what happened."

Right about then another officer walked up to our little group with a photo in his hand. "Mrs. Mercer, would you take a look at this picture from the security camera please? Does this look like Bobby?"

It did. Some lady had Bobby by the hand leading him down the hall. He appeared to be crying and trying to pull away. The woman acted like she was scolding him, like some parent or grandparent might do who had a tired, unruly child on her hands.

"Does anyone recognize the lady?" Sean O'Connor asked?

"I've never seen her before in my life," Ginny said.

Marty and I both took another look. Neither of us thought she looked familiar either. The lady appeared to be much older than Ginny Mercer—maybe in her early fifties? She seemed to be relatively well dressed, normal height and weight, and with no real outstanding qualities. In other words, she looked like just about anyone. The big question then became, why did Bobby go with her? Had she kidnapped him? Did she want to help him look for his mom? If so, why hadn't she reported it to mall security? They would have announced it over the PA system.

"Did anyone check the parking lot cameras?" O'Connor asked the officer who bought in the photo.

"Sgt. Morris has a couple of people checking them now. They were pretty sure this was Bobby from the description so they're looking to see if they can spot them out there getting into a car or anything," the officer responded.

We had nothing to do but wait. Sergeant O'Connor paid a lot of personal attention to Mrs. Mercer. He even rubbed her hand and told her that it would be okay. They would find Bobby. He would see to it. About a half hour later another officer came up with a new photo from the north parking lot security camera. He showed us a picture of the lady buckling Bobby up in the front seat of an older red pickup truck. No car seat meant she hadn't intended to have a young child riding with her that day. Bobby seemed to be still crying.

Marty and I both called our parents to let them know what was up and that we might be a while. Marty wasn't about to let Mrs. Mercer out of his sight even if O'Connor did seem to have her somewhat under control by then.

"What can we do to help?" I asked both of them as they sat there waiting for who knows what. Bobby was long gone from the mall. Somebody kidnapped him. Why?

"Nothing that I know of," Sergeant O'Connor said, "unless you want to follow Mrs. Mercer home and maybe stay with her for a while as we try to sort this thing out."

Marty piped up, "Why don't I take Mrs. Mercer home in my car and Jeremy can follow along with hers? I don't think she should be driving as upset as she is."

That made sense so that's what we did. Then we stayed with her until later that evening until she finally started to crash for the night. We planned to stay right there until Sean showed up with a lady officer around eleven. She had just come on duty and would stay at the Mercer's until morning so she could be there just in case the phone rang or anything else happened.

On our way home, we stopped at a drive through to grab a bite to eat. We were starved. Hadn't eaten since lunch at the mall. While silently munching on our burgers and fries, Marty and I must have been hovering on the same wave link. "I wonder if there's any way your step dad could be involved in this." I mentioned as we headed down the nearly deserted streets on our way home.

"I don't know. That's all I've thought about since we first walked into the mall this afternoon."

"Me too," I hated to admit. "Mr. Andrews always tells us in English class that, for the most part, there is no such thing as a coincidence, and I tend to agree with him. Of all the little kids out there to kidnap, why would the one that you babysit for be the chosen one? Mrs. Mercer doesn't have any money to speak of. She's a single mom with just a normal job. Whoever did it can't be looking for a big ransom."

"I know. Something else popped into my head a while back that I can't shake. Bruno told me one time when he was mad at me for some reason or the other that he would sell me to a child slave market. I thought he was just BS'ing me at the time, but I guess from what I've read on the Internet there really is such a thing. Kids can be sold as household slaves where they work for twenty hours a day keeping house, cooking, and all that. Then, some kids are sold as sex slaves to perverts."

"I wish you hadn't told me that," I said to Marty. "There is no way that Bobby could be sold as a house slave, but a kiddy porn sex slave is a possibility. I wonder if we should mention that idea to Sean?" I asked.

"I think I'd hold off on that one for now. We don't know if there is any way Bruno is involved or not," Marty said. "Besides, he wasn't weird like that; he was just mean and evil. I can't

42

imagine him getting someone to kidnap Bobby unless he was doing it to get back at me somehow. And that is definitely a possibility. If that's what he's up to, he'll probably kill Bobby and set it up somehow for me to find his body."

We sat in the driveway at home for maybe another half hour hashing out ideas. As farfetched as I hoped Marty's fear was, I could visualize Marty opening up his car in the morning and finding Bobby's slashed up, bloody body propped up in the driver's seat. Naturally, I didn't mention those thoughts to him. There were times I didn't know for sure if I were having a vision or an overactive imagination attack. Anyway, the longer we talked, the less sure Marty felt that Bruno had anything to do with it—and that was good. I almost think he tried to talk himself out of the possibility. "As much as Bruno hates kids, I just can't imagine him taking Bobby and keeping him around. If he did do it, you can bet that lady is the one who has to care for him until Bruno decides what the hell he's gonna do."

While we sat there in the car hashing out ideas, we talked about bringing Scott into the search.

I reminded Marty, "Remember that Bobby is sensitive to Scott too. Since Bobby can see and talk to Scott just like I can, I'll bet Scott could help find him. Scott really likes Bobby, and I know he would want to help."

43

"Sounds like a great idea to me. Maybe I'll get to know Scott this way too," Marty reflected.

"I don't know if I can get him to help, but it sure is worth a try," I said as I climbed out of his car and headed for the house. "I'll see you in the morning and let you know what happens after I call Scott. Oh, by the way, let's think about whether we want to let Sean know what we're doing. He knows all about Scott and all that, but I don't know how he'd feel about us sticking our noses in. We'll talk about that tomorrow."

Chapter 4

When I walked into the house, Mom and Dad were still both
up and wanted to know everything. I'd called them a couple of
times during the day just to check in, but hadn't given out many
details. It always happened kind of in between things that we
were doing, and I never had enough time. So, I started at the
point where we showed up at the mall and told them the entire
story. Obviously they were concerned on a number of fronts. They
worried about Bobby and Mrs. Mercer, of course, but they also
felt uneasy about Marty and me. Who knows what that nut case
might be up to!

"You should tell Sergeant O'Connor what you're thinking
about Bashore doing away with Bobby as a warning or just plain
more meanness to spite Marty," Dad said. "For some reason or
the other, that's the only thing that makes sense to me—unless
he wants to use him as some kind of hostage while he makes his
get-away."

"Hadn't thought of the hostage idea. Marty thought his murdering Bobby might be kind of a stretch, but then, that could be wishful thinking on his part. I know he's worried. Yet at times tonight when we talked about it in the driveway, it almost sounded like he was in denial—like that maybe Bruno wouldn't have anything to do with the kidnapping? I hope he's right," I said thinking that Bruno's involvement just sounded too much like a possibility that we couldn't ignore.

"You know," Mom said, "Marty internalizes everything that is said about Bruno. He blames himself for stuff that his stepdad does. I almost wonder if we should keep most of the Bruno speculation to ourselves and not mention him any more than necessary around Marty. I'm really kind of worried about him."

"I think if Bruno's involved with Bobby's disappearance, Marty just might run away and disappear," Dad said. "That wouldn't be good for him or anyone else. I agree with Mom. When we're around him, let's just act like we think Bruno's long gone and not at all involved. In the meantime, I'd contact O'Connor and let him know what we're thinking if I were you."

"Okay, I'll call him in the morning. In the meantime, I'm exhausted. It's been an extremely long day, and I need to get some sleep. Good night!" I said standing up and heading for my room.

"Good night, Son," Mom and Dad both said.

As soon as I walked in, I closed the door, dumped my clothes in a heap on the floor and crawled into bed. Staring at the ceiling, I called out softly, "Scottie, I need you. Scottie, get your ass here, now! Bring Mooshy."

"Yeah, yeah, Dude! What's up?" Scott grumbled from the foot of my bed sitting Indian style like always with Mooshy curled up beside him sound asleep. He looked half asleep himself.

"I swear," I laughed. "That Boxer of yours can fall asleep at the drop of a hat. How long have you two been here?"

"Just arrived. Mooshy and I had already crashed for the night when you called so he just didn't bother stirring. He more or less came as he was. So what the hell's the big emergency? What's going on?"

"Some crazy bitch kidnapped Bobby at the mall. No clue who she is or why she did it. She hasn't sent a ransom note or anything. We've got this feeling that sick bastard Bruno Bashore is somehow behind it. Marty's scared to death that he'll kill Bobby and then set it up for him to find the body. Now Mom and Dad are getting paranoid about Marty. They didn't say so, but I think they are afraid that if something like that really happened, he'd go off the deep end and hurt himself or worse."

"Oh, brother!" Scottie said under his breath. "I wonder if that creep is involved. So tell me everything that's happened so far?"

47

So, I told Scott step by step everything that had gone on. When I finished, Scott said, "Okay, go to sleep. I need to chew this over in my head for a while tonight, and I don't want you interrupting me. Just shut your eyes, roll over, and zone out. Mooshy and I won't bother you. I'll just climb into my old bed over there against the wall when I'm ready. See you in the morning."

When I woke up, I eased out of bed as quietly as possible. Scott and Mooshy had curled up together and were sound asleep and snoring in the other bed just like they did when they were alive. Back then, making the bed in the morning tended to be a complete makeover. Now, the two of them could sleep in that bed all night and then crawl out of it in the morning with it looking perfectly normal just like nobody had even as much as sat on it, much less slept in it. Amazing! I moved around my bedroom trying not to make any noise before heading to the shower. No sense waking them up yet. It was only nine o'clock. After brushing my teeth, checking for whiskers, and diving in and out of the shower, I headed back to my room. By then Scott and Mooshy were both up. Mooshy wanted attention as usual nuzzling up expecting his ears to get rubbed.

"Morning, guys," I said as I went in and started dressing. "Get any productive brain farts last night when I left you to your own inner cogitations? You realize how scary that is? Your mind has always been kind of a blank." Couldn't help harassing just a bit; Scott would figure something was wrong if I didn't.

"As a matter of fact, I did. However, I think you should check in with Sean first to see if they had any luck using their more conventional means. Let's face it, if the cops can solve this thing, that's a lot better than it would be if we did."

"I know," I said. "I'll call Sean right after breakfast.

Mom and Dad were just heading out when I came out of my bedroom to join the world for the day. They planned to meet up with Scott's parents aka Marty's for breakfast. I think they wanted to talk about Marty without him being there. I don't think that Jim Dad and Mom Sara knew of some of our concerns about Bruno yet.

While they scurried themselves around and prepared to go, Mom strolled out into the kitchen to tell me about their plans for the morning. At one point she had a startled look on her face and reached down and scratched Mooshy behind the ears rather absent mindedly as he stood there rubbing against her leg looking for more attention. She never said a thing about it. She just sneezed like she always did around Mooshy. She's allergic to dog hair.

All she said that could be taken with maybe a deeper meaning was, "Well, someone has to figure out how to find Bobby, and it doesn't really matter who. All I know is the sooner it happens, the better everyone will feel."

49

She looked right at Scott when she said it. We never really knew for sure exactly what she saw or sensed and what she didn't. She never said, and I never asked. I've always known she had some sensitivity, but I've never known how much. She didn't talk about it, much less admit anything. Like I said earlier, Grandma told me that her dad always tried to make her stifle that part of her nature when she was a little girl, and she never got over it. She grew up thinking something was wrong with her.

However, Mom never tried to curb my sensitivity. The only thing she ever did was tell me that certain visions I mentioned were my imagination and not to tell anyone about it—like when I saw my grandma in the rocking chair a couple of days after she died. I knew better. Grandma and I talked and she told me she loved me and that the sensitivity ran in our family on my mom's side. She said that they thought it was running out as the generations went by. However, I realized that I was living proof that it could still be as strong as ever. I never told mom about any more of my visions after that.

Before Marty came over, I figured I'd better call Sean and get that part of my day out of the way. When he answered, I filled him in on what we were thinking and asked him if he would be willing to soft pedal the Bruno aspect when Marty was around.

"First off, Jeremy, I don't really think that Bruno is anywhere around. I may be wrong, but there hasn't been a sign of him anywhere so I have no problem not mentioning him in front of

Marty. Secondly, we have a plan. We know she had a package from Hardings when she put Bobby in the seat and buckled him in."

"How'd you figure that out?"

"The security cameras picked it up. It sat right there on the ground outside of the door while she did it. We managed to get a face shot image of her so we're going in there to see if anyone recognizes her. Then we'll see if anyone remembers her being in the store yesterday and what she bought. If we can determine that, we'll know if she used a check or credit card. Then we can get her address from there. If all else fails, we'll run all the checks and credit card transactions for the day and check them all out. Once we have a name, we can check with the Bureau of Motor Registrations to see what kind of vehicle she drives. If someone owns an older red pickup truck, we're in business.

"The one thing we're trying to avoid right now is blasting the pictures all over the television and Internet if we don't have to. If we don't find him in a few hours, that's what we'll have to do. However, there's always the chance that if that happens, the person involved might run or panic and harm the child. So we're gonna give it a little time. We've kept Mrs. Mercer in the loop with all decisions and she's ok with everything for the time being."

"How are we going to know what's going on for sure?" I asked.

"When you say 'we' are you referring to you and Marty, or is there someone else involved?"

"I'm not sure what you mean?" I said playing dumb on purpose.

"Bull! I'm talking about Scott and you know it."

"He's right here listening in and laughing at you," I said.

"Meet me in the food court at noon," he said and then pushed the end button on his phone literally hanging up on me.

I called Marty and dragged him out of bed. I told him to get dressed, eat, and get his butt over here ASAP. While we waited, Scott went over the plan he dreamed up last night after I went to sleep. However, he wanted to give the police first crack at finding Bobby.

A few minutes later, Marty walked into the house. As soon as he did, I told him, "Marty, to start with, don't sit down on the stool in the corner. Scott has his ass parked in it. Mooshy is sacked out beside him so be careful where you walk."

"Well, hi to both of you," Marty said looking at eye level above the chair. "I sure wish I could see you and talk with you, but I can't so I guess we'll just have to make do with what we can do."

"Scott can hear and see you so that's no big deal. I'll repeat anything he says. Just remember when we're around other people, it's just the two of us."

"No problem there. People would think we were pretty weird if they saw us talking to thin air," Marty said.

"Your point? Jeremy is weird. So, tell him the plan," Scott said.

"Ok, Scott says to tell you the plan after reminding you how weird he thinks I am," I told Marty with a smile on my face while rolling my eyes. Some things just never change. "First off we are going to meet Sean O'Connor at the mall at noon. He's going to tell us of their progress to date. We want you to drive your car just in case we need to go to Plan B. If the police have no luck, you'll be driving while I focus on Scott."

"So, what exactly is Plan B?" Marty asked.

Scott and I took some time and laid out our idea for Marty just in case the cops struck out with their strategy.

When we met up with Sean at noon, he told us, "Well, that fizzled big time. The whole idea of tracing a check or credit card went by the wayside. She paid by cash. She only made one purchase; she bought a bra. You can't trace cash. Now we're back to square one. They're getting ready to blast out a huge Amber

Alert on radio, TV, and the Internet this afternoon as soon as they get it taped."

"Ok, here's what we're gonna do," I said without waiting for any more bad news. "Scott's right here with us. Marty's driving his car. We're gonna go to the north end of town and start working our way south. We'll cruise up and down all the main streets trying to find him."

"That's like looking for a needle in a hay stack," Sean interrupted. "We already have every officer in town keeping an eye out for a red pickup truck."

"Hold on! That's not what we're looking for. Bobby's sensitive to Scott. He can see him and talk to him. You didn't know that, did you?"

"No. How long have you known that?"

"Long time—long story. Remind me to tell you about some of it some time."

"Only some of it?"

"Yeah, enough about that for now. What Scott's gonna try to do is connect with Bobby telepathically. If he does, Scott will go into the house and find him and tell him that we're going to get him out. Then we'll call the police station and give you guys the location."

"Hey, anything's worth a try at this point. Our big plan sure didn't work," Sean said. "One thing, if you do find something and call, be sure to use a pay phone if you can find one. That way it can't be traced back to your cell phone. Nobody else on the force needs to know what you're doing."

"After we make our anonymous call, is it okay to call you on your cell phone and fill you in on whatever details we can?"

"Yes, I'd really appreciate that"

We went over the plan in detail again getting Sean's input, and then we separated. The four of us counting Mooshy headed out to the parking lot. It just might turn out to be a long day or two. Hopefully, it would be productive, but who knows. Sean still thought it was like looking for a needle in a hay stack, but he didn't have any better idea. Besides, time was becoming a factor now. We had to try to find him before that lady saw herself on television and did something really crazy.

Chapter 5

We headed out to the parking lot, and the three of us talked about how to proceed. Repeating everything Scott said for Marty's benefit started to feel a little more normal. Anyway, we coped. I don't know why, but it never ceased to amaze me how well Scott accepted Marty who now lived in his house with his parents. It was obviously not an issue with Marty either. I just wish that...

When we got into the car, Scott climbed into the back seat and sat in the middle with Mooshy beside him looking out the window—no seat belts again. He didn't need them. Mooshy loved to go for rides so he stared contentedly out the window for at least five minutes before he curled up and went back to sleep. Marty drove and I sat in the passenger seat. We headed immediately to the most northwestern point in town to begin our hunt. I turned around and watched Scott as he leaned back with his eyes closed and concentrated. I could always tell when Scott was totally focused. He wrinkled his forehead.

With Scott in the zone, Marty and I pretty much ignored him for a while as we situated ourselves comfortably in the front seats and started our slow tour of the city—up one street and down the next. We stuck to relatively main streets. We figured that if Scott picked up on any of Bobby's vibes, it would probably reach out quite a ways. Then we'd have to narrow our focus and zero in on whichever direction we needed to go.

We started out crawling slowly up and down the streets. If anyone paid any attention us, they'd probably figure we were casing the neighborhood. It happened to be one of the nicer sections of town. Houses were good sized and kept up. Lawns were manicured with a number of lawn service vehicles parked in the area. Many of the streets didn't even have sidewalks—looked like they'd probably planned it that way. This didn't really look like an area where someone might try to hide a kidnapped child, but who could ever tell for sure. We had to start someplace, and Sean said that one area would probably be as good as any other. He didn't have a whole lot of hope for our plan.

After about fifteen minutes, I interrupted Scott's concentration, "Scottie, what's going on in that head of yours now? You look like your mind's a million miles away."

"Stop the car for a minute, and I'll tell you."

Marty pulled over to the curb and turned off the engine. No sense wasting gas. "So clue us in," Marty told him.

"Like I told you at the house, I'm trying to connect to Bobby telepathically, sort of like the reverse of when you call me. I'm just not sure how far out the vibes reach. I'm sitting back in the zone visualizing Bobby's face in my mind. Then in my head, I keep saying, 'Bobby! Bobby! It's me, Scott. Talk to me with your head, not your mouth just like we did at the mall the other day.' I just keep saying it over and over. Not always exactly the same way, but that's the gist of it. Like Sean says, it's probably a long shot, but if Bobby and I connect, we'll go from there."

After we talked for a few minutes, Marty started up the car, and we headed out again slowly but surely. As the day progressed, we eventually worked our way out of the nice neighborhoods of the northwest and made our way southeast. Around four o'clock, we had to take a bathroom break and get something to snack on. Marty pulled into a local fast food joint while Scott sat in the car. He didn't want anything, so we didn't disturb him any more than we had to. Sometimes he would eat, and sometimes he wouldn't. Usually when he ate, the food just kind of appeared. I don't think he ever actually paid for anything. Don't know how he managed it. Don't want to know.

When we returned to the car, he appeared to be asleep. "Are you awake?" I asked only kind of pulling his leg. "Anyway, pay

58

attention. We just saw the Amber Alert on the television they have up on the wall in there. Scott, you've got to find him!"

"Ok, relax. I might have something. Get the car rolling and head east at the intersection up ahead, and don't be in any big hurry," Scott said without even opening his eyes. Mooshy sat up in the seat, totally focused and staring straight ahead. That was different—he normally slept through most everything we did. Wonder if he sensed something different?

Marty and I looked at each other. We just shrugged our shoulders and grinned. "Ok, here we go," Marty said as he started the car and pulled out of the parking lot. We both felt pretty excited but didn't dare talk because we didn't want to mess up Scott's concentration.

We started down a street that pretty much traveled due east about twenty miles an hour. Everybody passed us and probably thought we were stoned. Oh, well! We drove down the main drag, past the local hospital, and towards the far end of the town. This area seemed pretty seedy. Cars sat on blocks in driveways, there were some un-mowed lawns, and we also saw all kinds of trash and litter that we hadn't seen earlier in the day in the nicer neighborhoods.

"Turn left!" Scottie said suddenly, "Right now!"

"Hold your pants on!" I told him. "The corner's about a half block away."

Thirty seconds later we turned and headed north. We drove about two blocks when Scott told us to turn left again which headed us back to the west.

"Stop!" Scottie shouted out. Marty damn near put me through the windshield slamming on the brakes after I repeated it just as loudly and sharply as Scott. There we sat in front of a seedy looking house with a screened in porch that needed painting badly. The garage door stood open, and we could see an older red pickup truck parked inside.

"Bingo!"

"Go around the block and see if you can park directly behind this place and be out of sight. Do either of you have anything to write on? We need to jot down the address of this dump."

Marty pulled a pen out of his pocket while I grabbed a napkin left over from our snack run. I wrote the address down, and then we headed to the corner. I double checked the name of the street on the street sign at the end of the block. Someone had apparently hit the thing and bent it out of shape. Therefore we weren't exactly sure what street we were on. We drove another block to check out the next one. That one stood straight and undamaged. After all of that, we figured we had the correct address if nothing else.

We drove around the block and parked in front of an empty lot on the next street almost directly behind the house where Scott thought Bobby was located. As Scott and Mooshy started to get out, he told us, "You guys wait right here until I come back. Mooshy and I are going in that house to see if Bobby's in there and okay. Be right back."

"How you gonna get in?" Marty asked.

"Don't sweat the small stuff!" Scottie answered with a grin as he looked at me.

"Our angelic wonder boy can just walk through walls," I told Marty as Scott and Mooshy appeared on the outside of the car without opening the car door giving me a goofy crazed expression that I tried to describe as the two of them jogged off towards the house.

Marty and I had no clue as to what we should be doing so we just sat there and talked wondering what they found when they got there. Maybe ten minutes Scott appeared back inside of the car alone.

"Go make that telephone call to 911 and to Sean. Bobby's in there and he's okay. He and I talked telepathically. He's in good spirits now that he knows I'm here with him. Mooshy and Bobby are playing telepathically. Physically, he's walking around watching his shoes blink on and off. Mentally, he and Mooshy are rolling around together on the floor.

"Anyway, tell Sean that some crazy old lady's trying to brainwash him into thinking that she's his new mom. I'm going back there to keep Bobby and Mooshy company until the police come. I'll fill you in on all the details after Sean gets him out of there. The good news is, she doesn't have her television on."

He went through the door and disappeared again just that fast. While we had been driving around earlier, Marty and I took note of every pay phone that we passed. They're pretty scarce these days. The last one we remembered stood outside a carryout party store about a half mile away. When we found it again, Marty made the call. He dialed 911 and waited. It didn't take but a single ring before someone answered. Marty spoke in a low, raspy tone trying to camouflage his real voice, "Tell that kidnapping task force of yours that the crazy old lady I just saw on television who stole that little four year old boy, lives at 1902 Franklin Avenue."

He hung up without waiting for an answer just as we planned it. We knew that caller ID would instantly trace the location of the phone so we wanted out of there. We drove back to our parking spot in the next block north of Franklin. As soon as Marty stopped the car, I called Sean.

He checked his caller id before answering, "Jeremy the 911 call from dispatch just went out. There are a bunch of other cars besides me headed in that direction now. Good job, guys! Anything in particular that I should know?"

"Just that Scott said that it's some crazy old lady trying to convince Bobby that she's his mom," I answered him back. "Oh, also he said that she didn't have her TV on so she won't know she's been identified."

"Great! I'm almost there. Where are you?"

"Marty and I are parked one street due north of her house. We're in front of an empty lot."

"Stay there. Don't come snooping around to the front of the house when all the police cars show up. We don't need any of the other cops recognizing you and wondering what the hell you're doing there. Where's Scott now?"

"He went back to the house to stay with Bobby and Mooshy. He left Mooshy to play with Bobby and watch over things when he came back to tell us what was going on. Other than that, I don't know what's happening. He didn't take time to go into a whole lot of detail," I answered.

"Okay, I'll be in touch."

It must have been a half hour later when Scott and Mooshy appeared back in the car. Both acted emotionally exhausted. "We're gonna meet Sean at the food court at nine o'clock tomorrow morning. He's buying breakfast. It'll probably take that long for me to tell you everything. He's on the way to the hospital so Bobby can be checked out. Mrs. Mercer is gonna meet them there."

"So go back to the beginning," I told him. "Tell us everything from when you went in there the first time until now."

"When I first slipped into the house, Bobby stood there crying while stomping his feet. She tried to hush him up by telling him, 'You're my baby boy now. Your mom doesn't want you. She left you all alone at the mall. I'm your mommy now. You've got to call me Mommy.' Well, I caught Bobby's eye with my finger up to my lips like we always do and shook my head. He stopped crying almost immediately completely ignoring the dumb broad.

"I started telepathing to him, 'No, that's not true. Your mommy loves you. She did not leave you. Marty and Jeremy and I are all helping Sergeant Sean and are going to get you home. Be a real big boy and tell her, no, she's not your mommy.

"So he did. He belted it right out, 'No, you not my mommy. My mommy loves me. She's gonna find me.' I clapped and told him that he did a super great job and that Jeremy and Marty were going to call the police and they would come to get him and take

64

him home. After I had him all settled down, I came to tell you to call Sean. Before I left, I told Bobby exactly what I would be doing, and that he should just sit tight and not worry because I would be right back and wait with him until the cops arrived. I also gave Mooshy strict orders to keep him safe 'til I got back. He understood."

"So, that's when you originally came back and told us," I said.

"Right! So when I went back, I didn't see him at first so I connected with him telepathically. She had locked him in a bedroom '...until he could behave like a good boy and start calling her mommy.' As soon as I figured out which room she'd stashed him in, I just kind of moseyed through the wall and found him still playing with Mooshy. The three of us stayed in there until Sean and the rest of the cops showed up.

"While we waited, he told me that he heard me calling him, and that he'd answered a bunch of times. Weird, I only heard him the one time before I zeroed in on his frequency. Anyway, we practiced communicating and playing with Mooshy with just our minds while he kept a straight face or physically did something else like throw another little temper tantrum for her benefit while locked in the room. I put him up to that one, and it was hilarious.

"I kept telling him stupid jokes just to entertain him while he screwed around with Mooshy as we waited. It really blows my mind how Bobby can giggle and laugh telepathically while looking

65

sad and crying physically at the same time. He's really getting good at this. His mind is a regular little sponge. Whatever I tell him to try, he just does it. No big deal.

"When the police arrived, she tried to feed them some yarn about how there wasn't anyone there but her so I told Bobby to bang on the door and yell real loud. Sean walked over and unlocked the door that had the key still sticking in it. When he swung it open, Bobby flew out and jumped into his arms asking, 'Are you gonna take me home to my mommy?'

"Sean told him he would and then never set him down after that. What was funny was the way Sean kept looking around the room. I know he was trying to spot me, and I stood right there. Bobby looked at me and mouthed, 'I love you, Scottie. Please come and see me and bring Mooshy. I love him too.' I smiled at him and told him I definitely would. I picked Mooshy up in my arms and let them kiss each other goodbye. Mooshy even licked Sean's ear. Sean felt it too 'cause he wiped it with his hand.

"Before Sean walked out of the bedroom, he turned around in my general direction and mouthed so nobody else could hear him, 'Scott, food court 9 o'clock tomorrow morning. Bring Jeremy and Marty. I'm buying breakfast,' and then he walked out of the bedroom carrying Bobby.

"Anyway, what really topped the whole thing off happened in the living room before they left the house. Sean took out his cell phone and called Mrs. Mercer. 'Bobby,' he said, 'you want to talk to your mom?' Naturally he did. *Hummm!* I thought, finding it interesting that he had her number on his speed dial. Anyway, when she answered, Sean told her with no hint of anything in his voice that there had been some new developments in the case. Then he told her that he needed to have her speak to someone as he handed the phone to Bobby.

"Bobby chirped, 'Hi Mommy! I luv you. I gonna come home now.' Good Lord! I could hear her scream from the other side of the room.

"After a few minutes Sean finally pried the phone away from Bobby and told Ginny that they had to take him to the hospital emergency room just to have him checked over. It was standard procedure and that she should meet them there. Then he told her not to worry because if everything checked out okay, she could probably just take him home from there."

"Wow! That's quite a story," I said. "So have they all gone now?"

"Yes. After the phone call to Mrs. Mercer, Sean carried Bobby out to the car, strapped him in, and away they went. A couple of the other officers took that old bag out in handcuffs and put her in the back seat of their car and away they went off to city jail. She's a real nut case."

"Bruno didn't have anything to do with it then," Marty said with a sigh of relief.

"Nope, it was just this crazy old lady who wanted a kid. She saw Bobby wandering around by himself so she decided on the spur of the moment to steal him. Hopefully, now you can just forget about Bruno. He's out of here!"

We called both the rents to let them know Bobby was safe and headed home.

Thank goodness that ordeal was over! Bobby had made it home safe and sound and Bruno wasn't involved—time to go home and let down. Scott wasn't the only one who'd had an exhausting day. I could barely function, and I'm pretty sure that Marty felt the same. It had been an unforgettable day. However, the next day wouldn't get a whole lot better. Getting in trouble with Sean O'Connor wasn't my idea of fun.

Chapter 6

When I walked into the house, Mom and Dad were still
talking about Bobby. "Have you had your radio on?" Mom asked.
"It's all over the news. The police received an anonymous tip
about where someone was holding him. Apparently they arrested
some lady who sounds like she's maybe a bit deranged for
kidnapping."

"Yeah, Marty and I saw some of that going down. We'd
stopped at a burger joint and happened to see a whole bunch of
police cars racing down the street so like any red-blooded snoopy
teens, we followed—at a distance of course so we didn't get in
anyone's way." I said with a grin. "We parked down the street
with a bunch of other gawkers and watched. We had no clue
about what they were doing on until we saw Sean O'Connor walk
out of the house carrying Bobby. We hung around for a while and
watched them take out this old, old lady and put her in the car. It
was all pretty exciting. I bet you could hear Marty whoop from
here when he saw Bobby in O'Connor's arms."

69

"First off, that old, old lady is only forty-five," Mom said with a smirk on her face.

"And your point is?" I asked with my most innocent expression. After all, I had to give the old folks a little bit of grief when the opportunity presented itself.

"Smart aleck teenagers!" Mom snorted.

"Mom! You're hurting my feelings!" I faked.

"Right! You bet! So, were you and Marty the only ones in the car?"

"Yesssss," I answered slowly knowing darned well what she was implying. "Who else would there be?"

"Oh, nobody in particular. Just wondered," she answered with that darned knowing look on her face. Someday she's going to ask me about Scott point blank, and I'm not at all sure what I'm going to tell her when she does. I just hope that day never comes.

"In the meantime, I'm tired and gonna go to bed. Make sure I'm up in time to go meet Sean at the food court at nine in the morning. After the bust went down, Marty and I got a text message to meet him. He probably wants to tell us all about what happened. He knows how concerned Marty was about Bobby.

He's gotten really attached to him. He's more like an older brother than a babysitter."

"Ok, good night. Are you having breakfast here or with Sean?"

"He said he was buying breakfast so I don't have to be up much before eight-thirty."

It was about ten after nine when the four of us wandered into the food court. Sean sat there at a table all by himself. "I'm starved. It's about time you guys showed up."

"Well, there was a lot of traffic," Marty said. "So we drove very carefully just like always so not to cause any problems out there on the road."

"Excuse me a minute while I stick my head in the trash can and throw up," Sean said with a grin on his face. "Now, before it gets any deeper in here, let's go order."

When we made it back to the table, Scott and Mooshy had already started. What hogs! Both of them had pancakes, eggs, sausage and fried potatoes. Their dishes weren't showing either like stuff sometimes did when Scott held something. Don't know how he controls that. I'll have to ask him about it someday when I think of it.

When we sat down, Sean started by saying, "I really want to thank you guys for what you did yesterday. I don't know how you managed it, but I'm confident that Scott played an important role in the outcome somehow. Wouldn't like to tell me how you did it, would you?"

I looked over at Scott and he shrugged his shoulders and said, "Why not? He knows all about our connection anyway."

First off I told him that Scott and Mooshy were sitting right there at our table pigging down on their breakfasts. For a flash of an instant, Scott and Mooshy's plates full of food became visible, and then just as quickly disappeared. Marty and Sean both kind of gasped—wish I knew how the hell he did that! Anyway, after the initial shock wore off, I told him the entire story from start to finish about how we found Bobby. The tale blew his mind. I guess we all pretty much felt the same way. To think that Scott could telepathically zero in on Bobby at four years old and make him understand to focus back on him so we could locate him seemed awesome.

"Well, I guess that leaves me only one major cold case that hasn't been resolved yet," Sean said kind of wistfully.

"What case is that?" I asked.

"I still need to find that hit and run driver who killed Scott and fled. I just can't get over the idea that someone could just run

72

over a kid and then take off from the scene of the accident leaving him to die on the side of the road without trying to help out."

I paused for a moment and then became as serious as I could and said, "Sean, let it go! It's okay. Scott's okay with the way things turned out. I'm okay with it. We've both moved on knowing that what happened to him was acceptable under the circumstances. It couldn't have happened any other way so you have to just move on as well and not worry about investigating the accident any further. It doesn't need to be solved by you guys. Nothing good would come of it."

"You mean to tell me you two discovered what happened, and you didn't tell me or anyone else?" he asked a little hot under the collar.

"Yes!" I answered staring into his eyes.

"Yes? That's it? You aren't going to tell me anything else?"

"No! At least I don't think so."

"Marty, do you know anything about this?"

"No way! This is the first time I've ever heard any of this."

"Marty, you also realize, of course, that Mom Sara and Jim Dad must never hear about this as well, don't you," I asked, making it more of a statement than a question.

"You know I'd never tell a soul. You and I have too many secrets now that only the three of us know about to ever tell anyone. Besides, who the hell would ever believe us?"

O'Connor looked at me with his best cop glare, "Jeremy, you have twenty-four hours. You and Scott work it out between you, but at nine o'clock tomorrow morning I want the truth out of you one way or the other. We can either do it here or at the police station. What's it gonna be?"

"We'll talk it over and meet you here at nine in the morning with our decision," I told him.

"It is not fair to Scott's parents not to know. They agonize over this every time I see them. The only way they'll ever get complete closure is by knowing all the details."

After that we all stood up and left the table. It promised to be another long day. Marty took us home and dropped us off. I wanted to be by myself, with Scott of course, to work this out in my mind.

"Do we have any choice?" I asked Scott.

"Not really. I didn't really realize that Mom and Dad obsessed as much about the whole thing as Sean said. I just felt that Mrs. Mercer didn't need to be dragged into it since it was definitely an accident. No way will they ever arrest her so why put everybody through it?"

We spent most of the day holed up in my room or out riding around away from everybody so we could talk. It definitely turned into a long, long day.

The next morning Scott and I showed up right at nine a.m. Marty had to babysit, and this really didn't involve him. Sean sat there with a huge grin on his face when we walked in. It rubbed me a little bit wrong. Did he think he's won some big battle of wits or something?

"Hi, guys!" Sean beamed. "Everybody's off the hook. Last night we found out the truth. Scott's killer ratted on himself."

"Oh, n.. n.. no!" I stuttered. "How'd you find out? Has she been arrested?"

"She? No! He! And he's in custody. Yesterday a man walked into the police station and turned himself in."

Scott and I looked at each other, and then I said, "What? I don't believe it. You'd better tell us about this. It doesn't sound like what we planned to tell you at all."

75

"Very simple! The guy who hit Scott was drunk on his ass when it happened and coincidentally on parole. He knew that if he stopped, we'd of run a LIEN on him, and he would have gone back to jail. He didn't think he couldn't handle that. However, after he sobered up and got some help from AA to straighten out his life, his conscience got the best of him so late yesterday afternoon he walked into the police station and turned himself in."

"Do Jim and Sara know about it yet?" I asked.

"Yes. I met them at the department sanctuary along with the police chaplain early this morning, and we gave them the news. They're hugely relieved. When I said goodbye to them, they headed straight for your house to tell your parents. They should have all the details by now."

"Oh, boy! Did we have it wrong. Thank God!" I said with a huge sigh of relief.

"So how did you and Scott think it happened?" he asked.

"I assume you remember the story about how I actually met Ginny, don't you?" I asked.

"Yeah, but, what does that have to do with anything? Refresh my memory."

"Scott was already dead, and I'd been putting in my hours behind the wheel before I took the road test for my driver's license. I worked myself all up into a tizzy after running a stop sign with that idiot hooting on me in the back seat. I bailed out of our car in the middle of the road and walked home with him tagging along beside me. I left mom sitting in the passenger seat when I jumped out of the car. Needless to say, that didn't impress her one bit.

"Anyway, as we walked home the temperature started cranking up, and I got thirsty. We strolled by some house where a lady and her little boy stood around out in front watering her flowers. That's where I met Ginny and Bobby. That's also when I learned that Bobby's also sensitive to Scott when they started talking to each other.

"Like you already know, Bobby's dad died in Iraq and is buried near Scott. The two of them had met and had talked there at the cemetery several times previously whenever his mom visited his dad. His mom thinks he has an imaginary friend. She became all embarrassed about how Bobby was talking so Scott led him over to the car where they could talk between themselves."

"So what's any of this have to do with anything?" Sean asked.

"That's when Bobby pointed out the new dent in the door with the red paint on it. Scott got suspicious. It sounded like too much of a coincidence so he had me ask her how it happened. She told us that she thought it had happened in the emergency room parking lot."

"Am I getting the impression here that you thought Ginny Mercer killed Scott?"

"Yes! It all added up. She told me that it happened the same day that teen aged boy was hit by a car and killed and buried close by to her husband. It seems that Bobby climbed up on the cupboard trying to grab a real glass for a drink of water. He didn't like the plastic glasses she always made him use. Anyway, he fell, the glass broke on the sink on the way down, and Bobby ended up with a bad cut on his neck. She grabbed a wet towel for a compress and went hurtling towards the hospital as fast as she could."

"So how does this all end up with her killing Scott?"

"Right as she drove down the street where Scott was riding his red bike to the store on an errand for his mom, she told us that Bobby had a seizure from blood loss and shock. She said she grabbed him and knew she veered all over the road. We figured that she side swiped Scott at the same time without even realizing it."

"Oh, boy!" Sean sighed. "And you guys have lived with that thought all this time?"

"Yeah, combining what we knew and what we assumed, we knew he hit his head on the curb, broke his neck, and severed his carotid artery on a broken bottle all at the same time. For all intents and purposes, he died instantly. The way we had it figured, if Cindy Mercer had known she hit Scott, she would have stopped. If she'd stopped to help him or to tend to Bobby's seizure or for any other reason, Bobby would have bled to death. As it was, she arrived at the emergency room with less than five minutes to spare. Scott died and Bobby lived. We called it fate. Scott and I talked it over and decided that it would be our secret. We saw no reason for anyone else to ever find out the truth of the accident."

"Oh, boy! That's almost cruel that you guys have had this festering in your heads all this time. I wish you'd of shared, 'cause maybe I could have helped you somehow. However, I guess I understand why you didn't. At least now everyone knows the truth." Sean said shaking his head and actually feeling sorry for us.

Sean, Scott, and I talked for a little longer, but Scott wanted to get out of there and go check up on his parents. However, just before we left I had to leave one last zinger for Sean.

"Sean, I don't know if I should tell you this or not, but I guess I'm going to have to. Last night I had a vision or dream or something. Just before going to sleep, I was tossing and turning with all the day's activities running through my mind. I rehashed that part where you carried Bobby out of that lunatic's house and strapped him in the car. Then out of nowhere this vision kicked in and the scene suddenly jumped ahead about six years. Bobby looked to be probably ten years old. You, Ginny, Bobby, and two other little kids—one a girl about six and then another little boy about four were all walking to the car. Everyone was laughing about something. Then Bobby said real seriously like, 'Dad, the stories you tell the little kids are just plain terrible! They never know whether to believe you or not. Darned good thing Marty and I are around to keep them straightened out.' "

"Are you pulling my leg?" he asked very seriously.

"Not at all. You know, Sean, there's no sense putting off the inevitable," I said as Scott, Mooshy, and I all stood up and left the table laughing—leaving Sean sitting there with his mouth open and hormones raging. However, isn't it supposed to be the teenagers who are hassled with raging hormones? Hummm! Our turn was coming.

Chapter 7

Monday started a new marking period at school. Mr. Andrews brought over a new girl and sat her down with Marty and me. He introduced us around. Her name's Ashley Moore. She just moved into town. Her dad just changed jobs and by coincidence works at the same architectural firm as my dad.

With Mr. Andrews still standing at the table, Marty asked her with a smart alec look on his face, "Do you wrestle?"

"Depends," she said with a huge grin on her face.

We all laughed at that one. She's a doll—very petite, beautiful, and not at all athletic looking! With Bruno long out of the picture, Marty had started to show a sense of humor that I hadn't previously seen from him. He actually could be quite funny at times.

With this being the first day of the new marking period, Mr. Andrews passed out our new projects and explained them as he went. Therefore we had a lot of time to just chat among ourselves. It could be my imagination, but the longer the hour went, it seemed like the more the conversation directed itself to be between Marty and Ashley.

Wrestling practice started in two weeks so Marty and I planned to start running that evening after dinner to kind of get a head start on our conditioning. Both of us usually ate dinner around 5:30 when the dads got home so we decided to set out about seven. About five minutes to the hour, I texted Marty, "Ready?"

He responded with, "K," so I slipped on my Nikes and headed out to the driveway. Who should walk out of their house with Marty, but Ashley.

"Hey! Ashley's gonna run with us," Marty said as they jogged over to where I stood.

"Yeah, I went over to the Mercer's with Marty after school so we could do our homework. We have three classes together. How lucky is that? Anyway, I want to get into shape too. Hope you don't mind my tagging along. Just hope I don't hold you guys back too much."

"No problem! So how'd you like the kids?" I asked.

"They're both darling. Emily is such a little doll, and Bobby is such a sweet boy. I absolutely love both of them."

"She stayed until I left and then she went home to eat. She just now got back so she could run with us. Pretty cool, huh?" Marty explained.

Man! I didn't know about Ashley and the guys, but Marty sure seemed quick with the women.

It worried me a bit that she might slow us down, being a girl and all that, and I seriously wanted to get into some kind of shape before the season started. Ha! That concern lasted about thirty seconds. She mopped up the floor with us. She'd run cross country every year since the sixth grade and placed in the states last year as a junior. When we finished, I think Marty and my tongues both hung out. She'd barely broken a sweat.

"That was fun! Same time tomorrow, guys?" she asked.

"Yeah, sure!" We both answered. Good Lord, if that didn't provide motivation to get into shape, nothing would.

Friday in English class Marty told us, "I can't run tonight. I'm babysitting late for Bobby. Ginny and Sean are going out to dinner and then a movie. I told Ginny that I would do it as a freebee because I know that between day care and my babysitting, it's getting pretty tight for her."

"Hummm, Ginny and Sean? That's interesting. Anyway, that was decent of you," I said. "What'd she say?"

"She told me not to worry about the money because Sean planned to pay me. Apparently she's not even coming home from work long enough to change. He's gonna wait in the driveway while she runs in to say hi and goodbye to Bobby and then just jump into his car and away they'll go. Bobby and I'll take Emily home when Mom gets there, and then we'll come back and cook dinner for Bobby and me. Now, doesn't that sound domestic?"

"So, Ashley, are you running tonight?" I asked laughing at the domestic Marty image.

She kind of blushed and said, "No. I'm going to help Marty cook dinner for Bobby. Between the two of us we should be able to stir up something that tastes somewhat edible."

"Oh, oh! This is starting to look serious," I hooted as we separated.

Oh well, so I ran by myself—at a much more leisurely pace, I might add. The next two weeks went pretty quickly, and then it was time for practice to start. Couldn't help but wonder how Marty would do this year. He'd gained a lot of weight since the end of last year's season when he wrestled one weight below me. This year he'd be at the weight class above. Since he finally started eating like a normal human being, he'd popped a growth spurt.

Of course that wasn't the only question I had in my mind. How would it be for him to be able to actually concentrate on wrestling without Bruno standing against the wall glaring at him and then beating on him when he got home if he screwed up somehow during practice or during a meet? Would he be more or less driven? Wouldn't surprise me if he just quit—especially with Ashley on the scene. There were some things that we just didn't talk about too much. With Bruno still on the loose from the state mental hospital, he never strayed too far from Marty's mind. If he wanted to talk about him, we did. However, I never mentioned him unless Marty did first. I just wish that Bruno would somehow disappear out of our heads completely.

Friday night I had a text message from Marty, "Meet us at the food court at noon tomorrow."

"K" I texted back. I didn't have anything better to do. It should be fun. They probably decided to treat Bobby to a Saturday morning snack or something and wanted company. I hadn't seen much of either one of them since they started getting serious. They kept pretty much to themselves, and I hated playing odd man out.

When I showed up at the food court, they already had a table. Somebody else sat there with them, and it sure didn't look like Bobby. Walking down the aisle towards them, it looked like a chick. *"Hummmm,"* I asked myself. *"What's up?"*

I strolled over and pulled up a chair, "Hi, everyone. Hope I'm not late." I knew I wasn't, but they caught me by surprise with that other girl being there, so I had to say something even if it did sound stupid.

Ashley jumped right in, "Hi, Jeremy. No, you aren't late. Doesn't matter anyway," she stated sounding just a bit nervous. "Want you to meet my cousin Alexis, better known as Lexie. Jeremy –Lexie; Lexie – Jeremy."

We both said "Hi!" I felt just a little bit awkward and foolish. I really had no idea what they were up to or why. However, I was interested. She looked pretty damned hot to me.

"Lexie and I are first cousins. We were born real close together so our parents thought they would be cool and name us similarly so we be became Ashley and Alexis. Now isn't that just clubby? Actually, the way it's turned out, we've always been best of friends as well as cousins. She and her parents lived down in the southern part of the state for the past few years so I haven't seen that much of her. Fortunately, for me anyway, they've just moved into Holter. Their house is only about ten miles from ours so I'll get to see her more often now. Marty and I thought it would be fun to have the two of you meet."

We hung out for another hour or so before they had to go. Ashley and Alexis had plans to meet Lexie's parents somewhere at three. We traded emails and cell phone numbers and headed out.

"Marty, give me a call later or come on over when you get home," I said as we split up.

I hadn't been home for more than a couple of minutes when Marty pulled into their driveway. He headed right over. "We need to talk," he said as he walked in.

"Yeah, I guess. What's going on?" I asked. "That whole thing came down as a bit sneaky. I don't mind getting set up, but I would at least like to have some advanced warning—like, these jeans I'm wearing are pretty ratty looking."

"I know. I'm sorry. I really didn't know anything about it either until last night. Ashley told Lexie about you and she wanted to meet you. They planned and arranged the whole thing. Anyway, here's the deal with Lexie. She and her parents just moved in with Lexie and Ashley's grandmother. Absolutely nobody's happy about it; however, for right now that's the way it's gotta be."

"Why?" I asked. "That can't be good for anyone. I can see it the other way around when the grandparent gets old and needs to be taken care of and moves in with the adult kid, but to have

87

the adult kid and family move back in with the parent seems kind of weird."

"I know," Marty said. "That's why it's all kind of hush, hush in the family. Lexie's dad lost his job about a year ago and hasn't been able to find anything since. In the meantime, his unemployment ran out, the mortgage company foreclosed on their house, and that forced them to move. No job, no money, no home. Either they moved in with grandma or under a bridge someplace in a cardboard box."

"That sucks!" I said thinking back to when Dad only worked part time because of the recession. We thought we had it bad. Guess I didn't realize how lucky we were with the economy tanking the way it did. "So what are they going to do?"

"I guess he's out every day beating the bushes looking for a job. He's really getting depressed, and the whole family's worried sick about him. If he doesn't find something soon, they're afraid he'll go off the deep end somehow."

"So, then there is Lexie," I stated as I raised my eyebrows wondering just exactly what they expected out of me.

"Yeah, then there is Lexie. Actually Ashley and Alexis have always been 'fairly' friendly, as far as cousins go, but maybe not quite as close as Ashley pretended. Lexie's a little on the wild side. However, she really feels sorry for Lexie and their family and hoped that the two of you might hit it off. Lexie's really depressed right now too and needs something good in her life."

"And, I'm supposed to be that something good?"

"I know. Sounds corny, doesn't it? However, that's what Ashley's hoping for anyway."

"I guess I'm willing to try and all that, it's just the way it took me all by surprise, I guess. I mean, like, she's really good looking and all that, but it's like she was dumped on me. 'Here you go, Jeremy. Here's your new girlfriend, Alexis.'"

"Oh, come on! It's not quite that bad," Marty laughed.

"I know. Why don't we do some kind of a double date and see if things work themselves out."

"Ok, we'll have to work around wrestling and babysitting. I'll let the girls work it out. And, oh, by the way, thanks!"

Now, speaking of raging hormones, life was about to get more interesting. I've heard that the older you get, the less things surprise you. However, ...

Chapter 8

Our first official practice started on November 16th. It seemed good to be back at it again. The first two weeks of practice are weed out times for most sports. People will go out for a team having no idea what they're getting themselves into. One of the neat things about wrestling is the fact that the coaches never cut. They just make practice so brutal, unmotivated people, who shouldn't really be there, drop out on their own.

After a week and a half of practice came a four day break from school during the Thanksgiving weekend. Of course, that didn't count for wrestling. Coach scheduled practice on both Friday and Saturday. After all of us stuffed our faces to the gills on Thursday, I guess we probably would need it.

Thanksgiving started out just like every year. Our two families always get together at either our house or the Adams's. It really doesn't make any difference because the two moms just do everything together anyway. This year dinner just happened to be at our house. Sara showed up around ten in the morning so that they could get a head start on the preparations. Marty and Jim Dad showed up at noon. That's when the Lions and the Packers kick off their annual Thanksgiving bash—which I think is an unintended pun meaning that the Lions will get their brains bashed in—again! The moms planned dinner for about one thirty which pretty much coincided with half time, which, incidentally, had the Lions down 21-6. Obviously, it would not be a major problem if we missed part of the game during dinner.

When we sat down to eat, Mom still had this silly grin on her face. She'd worn it for a couple of days, and I had no idea why. I actually asked her about it the day before, and she wanted to know what my problem was. Couldn't she be in a good mood? I shut up.

By the time the moms served desert, the game had stretched well into the third quarter. Marty and I were getting a little antsy to catch the end of the slaughter. That's when Mom dropped the bomb.

"Oh, by the way," she started. "Before the guys go racing back to the game or anything, I have a little announcement. I'm two months pregnant. Just found out officially Thursday. Looks like the due date will be late June."

I think my jaw hit the table. Everyone started talking at the same time asking questions and congratulating Mom and Dad.

The only other person at the table who knew the news in advance was Dad. He just sat there and grinned. Mom said she thought that menopause had kicked in and decided she should touch base with our doctor. He did a couple of quick tests and told her that she was pregnant and needed to get her into contact with an obstetrician. She knew exactly who she wanted. She wanted Dr. Lloyd Malcolm, the old codger who delivered me. According to Mom, our family doctor didn't act too wild about the idea because Dr. Malcolm didn't adhere to all the really modern ways of doing things, but he still practiced, and that's who she wanted.

"Have you had an ultrasound yet?" Mom Sara asked.

"No! I told the doctor I wouldn't have one. I don't want to know anything about the baby until he or she's born. I want all the details to be a surprise to me along with everyone else. If I had the test, someone might accidentally let the cat out of the bag. I told the doctor that as long as the baby appears to be healthy and growing in there, I don't want to know anything— nada! I just want to be surprised. I swore him to secrecy."

I didn't even know what they were talking about with all those tests she mentioned. I really didn't care. All I knew, I was going to have a little baby brother or sister, and I really didn't give a rip what it turned out to be. I didn't care, but I'd still kind of like to know what it's going to be, though, before it's born. However, I did know when to keep my mouth shut—some times. Mom sometimes acted kind of strangely when it came to certain things, and I guess knowing the sex of her baby in advance would be one of them.

She did share some concerns though, "I wonder if I'm too old for this. Eighteen years between babies is a long time. I won't know how to act."

"Nonsense!" Sara piped up. "I waited seventeen years between Scott and Emily and everything went fine."

"Oh, I know. It's just that getting ready for a new baby after all this time is going to be overwhelming. We gave away all of Jeremy's baby stuff years ago. We don't even have an old diaper pail lying around anyplace. I think we threw that away when he hit ten or so," she smirked while everyone laughed at me as I turned red. "We'll have to start totally from scratch."

"Not really," Sara added as the two women started planning in earnest while the rest of us more or less just sat there and listened. "Emily will be almost a year and a half when the baby arrives and she'll be ready for a youth bed so you can have her bassinette and crib. Seems only fair—you bought the bassinette for her when she was born. There's a lot of other stuff that she's outgrown too that we might as well get some more use out of. We sure won't need the stuff again. Jim made sure of that," she said giving Jim Dad his turn to blush.

"Well, I certainly know what my Christmas list is going to look like this year," Mom laughed. "Let's see now, diapers, baby bottles, blankets, little outfits appropriate for boy or girl, pictures and toys for the nursery. And that's just off the top of my head. Think what that list will look like by the time I get to sit down and actually write it out."

Everyone laughed, but for some reason or the other, I couldn't imagine myself getting Mom a diaper pail for Christmas. I'd just have to work on that idea.

By then we completely forgot about the game. In fact, I had to check ESPN.com later to find out the final score. We hadn't missed a thing. The big news of the day was the upcoming baby. The two moms rambled on and on and on. Marty and I pretty much sat there speechless and just listened, looked at each other, and rolled our eyes periodically. Dad had this big Cheshire cat grin on his face as Jim Dad looked over at him and said, "Stud!" under his breath.

The moms disappeared, and the dads whispered at each other, elbowing, and laughing like a couple of thirteen year olds. They tried to act real secretive like Marty and I didn't know what caused the big event or something. Oh well, not a big deal. We didn't have anything better to do—we cleaned the kitchen. By the way, scrubbing turkey roasters is a pain in the butt. I guess that it was close to six o'clock before everything calmed down, and they started packing up to go home.

When everyone left, Mom made hot chocolate, and we sat down at the table in the kitchen. She asked me what I really thought about having a new little brother or sister in the family. I told her I thought it'd be cool, but to remember, "I don't do poopy diapers!"

She just smiled at me and said, "Right! Seems like I've heard something about that before—like maybe when Emily was born?"

"Mom, what do you want? Do you care?"

"No, not really. I'd like to have another boy because I'm so used to having boys around, and I like them. However, Emily has been lots of fun too. I wouldn't mind having those fussy little pink dresses either. I guess it really doesn't matter as long as the baby's healthy."

I couldn't wait to get out on the patio by myself and call Lexie. That little chat sucked! She thought it absolutely stupid that anyone Mom's age would let herself get pregnant.

"She's only thirty-eight," I told her. "It's not like she's a dinosaur or something."

"How are you going to feel to be seen walking through the mall or at the grocery store with her?" she asked. "You're going to be embarrassed out of your mind to be seen with some fat cow waddling along beside you."

"Oh, Lexie! You're so over dramatic! It's not a big deal the way you're making it out to be. In fact, I think it's kind of exciting."

"Well, I still say she's way too old. You do realize what that's going to do to your relationship with your parents, don't you? You're gonna be odd man out. It will be Mom, Dad, and the baby. Oh, yeah. Somewhere out there is that other kid, Jeremy."

"I don't really think so. Anyway, I need to get in the house and do some homework. Just wanted to tell somebody about it. Talk to you later?

Well, that certainly turned into a downer. Here I am all excited and wanting to share the news, and all I hear is how stupid she thinks it is.

"Scott, Mooshy, check in!" I call out telepathically.

"Yeah, Bro! We're right here. Pretty exciting, isn't it? Why'd you even call that loser?" Scott chirped. How he always managed to show up so fast absolutely amazed me. This time I think he might have been already there just waiting to be called so he could make his appearance. Oh well, didn't matter. I needed someone to talk to.

"You know!"

"Well, yeah. Those of us with angel wings and halos know all," Scott laughed.

"Excuse me while I puke!" I said faking retching over the edge of the chair.

"You know what it's gonna be?" I asked.

"Nope! Haven't had time to check in on that little detail yet. Wouldn't tell you if I did."

"Why?" I asked.

"You aren't on the 'Need to know' list," he said giving me a hard time as usual.

We spent a while talking about the prospect of having a new baby and all that entailed. After an hour or so he had to leave.

Getting back to school on Monday kind of got my life back to normal. At least Jamie, my lab partner in chemistry, sounded excited about my news. She wanted to know all about it and thought it was absolutely wonderful. Jamie and I spend an awfully lot of time talking during our labs, but that's okay too. She's so darned smart we can talk all hour and still get our work done.

We had another full week of practice before we had our first meet. The first two weeks of the season went relatively easy. We had one meet a week for the first two weeks. After that, we had our first Saturday tournament. Ashley took over Marty's babysitting duties when he couldn't take care of the kids during the wrestling season. She wanted to bring Bobby and Lexie to the first Saturday event. He loved it and ran around all over the place.

Not so sure about Lexie. At least she smiled a lot and looked good as she checked out all the guys in their tight wrestling outfits. Mom and Dad came early but drove separately from Mom. Sara and Emily planned to arrive about the same time. Mom Sara wanted her car there in case Emily got fussy and she had to take her home for a nap. Jim Dad had to work until noon and then he'd show up.

About ten o'clock Mom Sara called Mom to let her know she'd be a little late. She'd been in a weird fender bender. Nobody got hurt in the thing, but it really shook her up. As she pulled out of the driveway, the brakes went out. The car rolled backwards right across the street and hit a telephone pole with her foot smashed to the floor on the brake pedal. Her front airbag went off right in her face. That scared her worse than hitting the pole. She'd called Jim Dad, and he'd come home to take care of the situation. They towed the car, even if it weren't damaged all that badly. They had to get the air bag reinstalled and check the brakes.

When they finally arrived, Dad and Jim Dad huddled together for quite a while. Finally, when I had a break between matches, I cornered Dad. "What's going on?" I asked. "Seems like a lot of kind of secretive talk between the two of you. What really happened out there with Mom Sara's car?"

"Jim is no mechanic, but the tow truck driver said it seemed like maybe somebody tampered with the brakes. The little line that runs brake fluid to the master cylinder looks like somebody messed with it. It appears bent like someone forced it off. The question is, did someone intentionally take that line off and drain the brake fluid out?"

"Like Bruno?" I asked.

"That's what Jim and I talked about. A police investigator will check it out with the mechanics at the repair shop so we should hear something definitive later. Don't say anything to Marty, please! He's shook up enough just knowing they had the little fender bender. If he thought something else might be going on, he'd lose it mentally. He's fragile, Jeremy, we have to protect him."

"I know. Fortunately Ashley and Alexis both came so he's going out there on the mat and doing his very best trying to show off for them. I don't think he's even considered Bruno in this since he's been out of the picture so long."

"I hope you're right, and you have to admit, Marty and Ashley are awfully kind of funny together. I don't know which one of them has it for the other the worse," Dad said.

"Dad, it's called hormones! It's the latest craze," I told him as he playfully backhanded me on the shoulder.

The Saturday meet went well. Ashley and Lexie took Bobby home when Ginny got home from work around five thirty. After dinner she and Sean brought Bobby back for the evening session. Marty and I both won first places in our weight classes, and Dad, Jim Dad, and Sean all huddled for most of the evening session down against the wall at the far end of the gym while the girls cheered us on. None of the adults seemed the least bit interested in sharing what they talked about so I didn't push the issue.

After we got home, Marty suggested that the four of us go for a ride just to let down from all the day's excitement. Between the accident and the tournament, we could use a little unwinding. Marty headed straight for the gravel pit. All the teenagers in town go there to make out and whatever, and I know that Marty and Ashley had parked out there several times in the past. That's okay. Time to find out just how friendly Lexie wanted to be. Would she want to make out or just talk? After all, it was kinda like our first date away from the mall, fast food places, or the wrestling meets.

After we parked, Marty and Ashley took the lead. They turned around and started talking like we were a pair of old married couples floating on the lake in a pontoon boat or something. I had my arm around Lexie, but that's as far as it went. Not exactly what I had in mind. We only stayed about a half hour when they decided we should leave because Marty had to babysit in the morning so they couldn't be out late. Duh! Why'd we even come?

On the way home Lexie whispered in my ear, "You know, it's still really pretty early. When we get back, why didn't we grab your car and come back out to the pits? We'd have more fun with it just being the two of us."

"Agreed! That'd have to be more fun than what just happened."

When we got back to town, Marty dropped Lexie and me off at the mall where I'd parked my car and away we went. As soon as I backed into our little space near the woods so the car faced the water, Lexie said, "Let's get in the back seat. There's a lot more room back there, and we don't have to fight the steering wheel or the console."

"Ok, let's do it," I said thinking that we just might get in some serious making out. I never had a real girlfriend before Lexie so I wasn't sure what would happen. I'd always been so involved with work, sports, practice, and school, that I never had time for girls.

We hadn't any more than gotten ourselves situated when she reached over and took me in her arms and started kissing me passionately. Next thing I knew she slipped her tongue between my lips and into my mouth. Pushed into the corner of the back seat, I started getting aroused and excited as she crawled all over me rubbing and grinding against my body.

We hadn't been there more than ten to fifteen minutes when she reached between my legs, rubbed her hand up my crotch and grabbed for my zipper. "Jeremy, I want you, and I want you now!"

"Whoa! Hold on! We can't do anything like that. I don't have protection with me," I stammered knowing I sounded like a complete idiot. Suddenly this whole thing was going way too fast and I wasn't ready.

"So? Who cares? You aren't gay are you?"

"No, but I do care about what happens to me. There is no way I'm going to take a chance on getting you or anybody else pregnant while I'm still in high school."

"Jeremy, I'm sorry! We'd better go. I don't know what got into me. It's just that you're so hot I couldn't help myself," she said as we both opened our doors and climbed out.

"Let's just walk down to the water and cool off a little before we leave. Okay?" I suggested as I headed down to the edge of the water at the pit.

"Jeremy, promise me. You won't tell Marty about what happened. Please! I really don't want him and Ashley to think badly of me."

"I won't say anything. Let's go ahead and start back to the car and get out of here before either one of us change our minds again."

We didn't talk a whole lot on the way back to town. I guess both of our minds churned a million miles away. Not only had I never had a real date before, I'd never had a girl literally attack me. Hot? I was hot okay, but not the way she meant. I'm just a normal guy. I'm not someone that all the girls salivate over. What the hell just happened? Why would she try to get it on with me fifteen minutes into our first real date alone? Nothing made any sense.

When I dropped her off at her house in Holter, I didn't even kiss her goodbye. I walked her to the door, told her goodnight, and left. I didn't know if we would see each other again or not. She probably wouldn't want anything to do with me after that deal. I didn't know for sure if I wanted anything to do with her. I had a ton on my mind and nobody to talk to. I'd call in Scott, but this didn't relate exactly to an emergency. However, I had to talk to somebody about it. Who?

Chapter 9

The next day in chemistry, Jamie Austin, my lab partner, who is just brainy as hell, stopped in the middle of the experiment we were working on and looked at me, "What's going on, Jeremy? You're totally distracted. You mind's nowhere near this lame experiment. You aren't worrying about the baby or anything, are you?"

"I'm sorry, Jamie. I guess you'd call it woman trouble."

"Care to tell me what's up?"

"You want the short version or the long?" I asked.

"Give me the long one. These chemicals have to simmer on low for twenty minutes before we can do anything else anyway," she said smiling.

She has the nicest smile. We've known each other since the seventh grade. We've always been friendly, but I've always been just a little bit intimidated by her because of her brain. She'll probably end up at the top of our class when we graduate.

When I finished telling her the whole story, she asked, "Do you think she told you the truth about getting all carried away or do you think she's a little slut? You know, there's another possibility too. Is she already pregnant and looking for a convenient 'daddy'?"

"Crap! I just don't know—hadn't thought of that. You know, I do feel kinda sorry for her because of her home situation, but I really can't say that I actually like her all that much. If it weren't for Marty and Ashley, I probably wouldn't even go out with her. It's not like she's a rag to look at or anything like that, she's actually darned good looking. I just don't think our personalities click."

"Give it some more time. Just make sure that you don't get caught with her alone. If you go to the pit with her by yourself again, you'll end up having sex with her whether you want to or not. Believe me. She'll show you a half empty birth control pill container, and convince you she's safe. You won't have an excuse."

We talked until the end of the hour. When the bell rang, I looked over to her and said, "Thanks, Jamie. You've been a big help. You've really given me a lot to think about."

"Jeremy, you can call me anytime you want to talk. I know you don't want to talk to your parents about any of this so that leaves Marty, and you've been sworn to secrecy as far as he's concerned. Scott would have been the perfect one for you to bounce ideas off of, but, you know... I'm sorry I brought Scott up, but I have been wondering how you are actually handling things. God! That had to be tough!"

"Better, I think. And thanks for the offer to talk. I'll probably take you up on it."

"Ok, see you tomorrow," she smiled as we each headed off to our next class.

"Bye!" Damn! I like her smile. She just seems so sincere and natural. I don't think there's a phony bone in her body.

That night, as I lay in bed thinking, I didn't know what to do. I let my friends set me up with a girl that I don't even really like, and I'm expected to date her and treat her like a girlfriend just because everyone feels sorry for her. Well, I feel sorry for her too, but that doesn't mean I want to act like I'm madly in love with her because I'm not. My God, she almost raped me yesterday on our first so-called date!

I need a normal girl friend where we can go out and have fun and not get too serious right away at least until we get to know each other a little better. I'm not ready for that. Marty and

Ashley's relationship is exactly what I'm looking for right now. They hang out together, have a lot of fun, and enjoy each other. Who knows what they do when they're alone. I don't care. That's the way it's supposed to be. If one thing leads to another, well, hell, so be it. However, her trying to climb my bones fifteen minutes into our first date scares the crap out of me.

Right then and out of the blue I heard this insane laughter at the foot of my bed. "Ahhhh, ha, ha, ha, ha! You are a total piece of work! Lexie tried to crawl into your boxers and you totally freaked! Ha, ha, ha, ha!"

"Scott! What are you doing here?"

"I came by just to hassle you, Bro. Why'd you let yourself get into that position in the first place?"

"Were you spying on us?"

"I couldn't! The windows were all fogged up so I couldn't see in."

"SCOTT! There's no way you're gonna sneak around and spy on me that way. Suppose I would have had a real girl friend out there and we had gotten on with it. Do I have to worry about you snooping then?"

107

"Relax! You forget that my job is to protect you and guide you through your fragile years. You keep forgetting that I'm your guardian angel. I have to watch over you."

"I'm gonna puke if you keep that up and I'll aim it right at the foot of the bed!"

"Go ahead, but remember, you're the one who will have to clean it up. Explain that one to your mom. She'll accuse you of drinking again. Seriously, though, if things had gone any farther I would have rigged up a police siren or fireworks, or something to somehow stop you. Jeremy, that girl's nothing but trouble. She's a bitch! And you've got to get yourself out of that mess. In the meantime, relax. If you're with a normal girl and have a normal relationship, you don't have to worry about me. I won't be babysitting you then."

"Thanks. I hope I don't have to look over my shoulder for the rest of my life to see if you're watching me. That could get embarrassing, you know. In the meantime what do we do about Lexie? I really want to get out of this relationship, and I don't know how."

"The first thing you have to do is make sure that you don't let yourself get trapped alone with her in some place like the pit. That's just asking for trouble."

"That's what Jamie said. She told me that Alexis would probably bring her half empty pill container with her next time just to make sure I didn't have an excuse."

"And Jamie's right! Incidentally, isn't that the same Jamie you've been flirting with since the seventh grade?"

"Same Jamie, yes, but I haven't been flirting with her since the seventh grade, Scott. We're just friends, and that's all we've ever been."

"Jeremy, are you really that freaking stupid? She's a nice girl, very bright, friendly, and has always secretly had the hots for you. Why don't you just ask her out? Then you could tell dear Lexie that you've found someone else, goodbye, and have a good life! Problem solved. Duh!"

"Scott, that'd be cool as hell, but Jamie's not gonna go out with me. She's way too smart. Good Lord! She's probably going to be our Valedictorian. What on earth would she see in someone like me?"

"In the first place, and I hate to have to admit it in front of you, but I guess I have no choice—except for when it comes to women and your total lack of any common sense, you really aren't all that stupid. You may not be the Valedictorian, but you won't end up riding at the rear end of the garbage truck either.

109

You're friendly, and you're really kind of an overall good kid. She'd probably love to go out with you.

"You could actually start by meeting her at the food court after school sometime in the near future so you could talk to her some more about your Alexis problems. Give her a line of some kind—it's more private, other classmates can't listen in, you won't be interrupted by having to boil gunk in some test tube or something, yada, yada, yada! Use your freaking head! Get creative, Bro!"

That might not be an all bad idea. Tomorrow the four of us are meeting at the mall for cokes after school so maybe Lexie will give me something else to talk about when Jamie and I do get together.

...

We'd been parked at our table in the food court talking for about a half hour when Marty looked over at me and said, "Hey! Feels like I've been sitting on my butt all day. Why don't we take a walk down the mall? They might be starting to get the new spring stuff in now. We can always check out which Bikinis would look best on our ladies."

"Why not? Let's go," I said as the four of us stood up, dumped our empty drink cups and started down the mall to where all the teen stores were located.

As we passed Gettleman's, Lexie stopped and exclaimed, "Oh, look! Those jeans are on sale for only $110 dollars. They'd look so hot on me. Jeremy, would you buy them for me? I really want 'um bad. Would you? Please? You could get them for me for Christmas."

I figured she was kidding, but she didn't act like it. "Right! You bet! Like I have a hundred and ten dollars plus tax just lying around. Sorry, Lexie. You want those jeans you're gonna have to get a job."

"You could get the money if you wanted to," she pouted suddenly getting all sullen. "Your parents have it. Mine don't. We're poor. All you'd have to do is ask."

"Afraid not, Lexie. First off, I don't ask my parents for a whole lot of money for myself, much less for friends. Dad gives me my allowance of twenty dollars a week and Mom gives me ten for gas, and that's all I get unless they just happen to buy me something on their own. Unfortunately, my buying the jeans for you is way out of my league. I'm having enough trouble trying to save up a little money to get my Mom and Dad something for Christmas as it is."

Apparently she really meant it, because she stayed in her major sulky mood. "Well, if you won't get them for me, I guess there is always the old fashioned way, eh Ashley?"

"What are you talking about? I'm not following you one bit," Ashley said with a puzzled look on her face.

"Oh, you know, the way we girls always do it. Take three pair into the dressing room to try and bring two out with the pair you want on underneath your own pants."

Ashley got a little hot on that one, "I don't think so, Alexis. That's stealing and that's something I just don't do or put up with. Make damn sure you don't do something like that when I'm with you."

"Oh, chill! I'm just kidding, and you know it," Lexie said.

Somehow I had the feeling she wasn't kidding. I don't think anyone else thought so either, but nobody said any more about it. Time would tell on that score.

Chapter 10

The following week we had our big rivalry meet with the other high school in town. We had big time competition with them in all sports. In the fall they'd won the football game so I imagine they planned to sweep the winter sports as well since they also won the basketball game the previous week. So for guy's sports anyway, the wrestlers had to win to bring home the glory in at least one of the major sports. Problem is, we wrestled in their gym. That put us at a disadvantage right up front.

Needless to say, practice all week zeroed in on one thing— where we could put people to be at the best advantage? Coach scrambled a bunch of our weight classes moving people up or down a weight to set up a competitive advantage. He didn't care if you went up a weight; however, he wouldn't let you actually cut weight and move down in an unhealthy way.

"You know," Marty said one afternoon after practice, "Everyplace I've competed at before has always been a lot more dog-eat-dog than Coach." He still hadn't gotten used to the way Coach Andrews did things.

"How's that?" I asked.

"All my other coaches always wanted and expected everyone to cut to the absolute minimum—no exceptions. The philosophy is, if your normal weight happens to be one-fifty, then you should wrestle at one-thirty five. That will give you the ultimate advantage."

"That's not the way Andrews does it," I told him. "He says that you should wrestle as close to your natural weight as possible. He feels that's where you're the strongest, healthiest, and feel your best physically and mentally. If you can beat the guy one weight up easier than the one at your weight, go for it. But you aren't gonna cut a couple of weights just so you can beat someone."

"Yeah, but you're probably gonna lose some matches sticking to the rules that way," Marty more or less ranted.

"Not necessarily. He thinks it's a lot more important for everyone to compete and have a good time than it is to win at any cost. I know he wants to win, but he wants it to be a good and memorable experience for us too."

"That just doesn't sound like much pressure to me. How you gonna get that competitive edge and killer instinct? Last year I got it from Bruno, but this year I'm not getting it from anyone."

"That's because he thinks that's your responsibility! The only thing he ever asks of us is to be physically fit, mentally prepared, and to do our best. If you come off the mat defeated, he doesn't turn it into a federal case as long as you gave your best effort. However, you better not ever just give up or slack off."

"Why? What'll he do then?"

"It's not what he'll do, it's what you'll do—laps, pushups, and all kinds of other little 'motivational' techniques he has up his sleeve. Maybe you didn't notice last year, but he used them a few times on a couple of seniors, and I don't want any part of them. I'll keep myself fired up for each and every contest," I told him. He hadn't seen that part of Coach Andrews yet. He had been so busy worrying about what Bruno said and did, he pretty much missed what else went on.

When we jogged out of the locker room Thursday evening to run our laps around the mat and then warm up, a stuffed dummy lay on the edge of the mat over near our seating area.

"Marty, look at that! It has big black X's for eyes and the letters J. W. painted on the chest. J. W.—Jeremy Wright. Hey! That's me."

"That's wild!" Marty laughed. They had patched together this caricature that supposedly looked like me all beaten up and lying on the mat in our corner.

"Priceless! I want it," I told Marty. "At the end of the meet, win, lose, or draw we take it."

Last year I won my match and that had been the turning point of the meet. I should've lost that match if you went by our records. If I had, they would've won by a narrow margin. By my squeaking out a victory, we squeaked out a win. Must be they remembered and thought about paybacks.

Coach figured that the meet could go either way again this year. If we could catch a break or two early on, we might be able to pull it off. One thing seemed for sure, we would probably start off with a loss. Our freshman ninety-eight pounder, Tom Harris, tipped the scales at 85 pounds soaking wet. He'd wrestled two years in middle school, was tougher than nails, but just not big enough for the lightest weight class in high school. Everyone on our team felt half jealous of him. He ate like a horse, never watched his diet, gorged on junk food, and never gained any weight. Not fair!

Their 98 pounder placed sixth in the state meet last year as a junior. According to the stories we heard, he normally spent most of the morning running and spitting on meet days so he could make weight. Heard rumors about diuretics and enemas too, but had no clue how true any of that might be. If he had been on our team, he would have wrestled at 105 or 112. Coach wouldn't put up with anybody misusing his body or taking any chances with their health.

Before the match started, Coach had Tommy at the corner of the mat with both hands on his shoulders, staring him in the eye, and talking turkey to him. This was more than a last second pep talk, they were plotting something. At the sound of the whistle, Tommy literally dove in for a flying leg tackle. It surprised the other kid so much, he landed on his back. Tommy scrambled up the kid's body, threw in a half nelson, and pinned him in approximately 20 seconds. The fans on our side went nuts. That stunt was totally, totally unexpected and totally awesome. Coach put him up to that flying tackle routine, and it worked. Sometimes he was a genius.

Their team and fans went into shock. That kind of thing during competition can be infectious. Their next kid suddenly didn't know what to expect, and ours had been given a jolt of adrenalin and confidence realizing that anything was possible. By the time they got to Marty and me, our team had won four out of five matches. I won and then Marty pinned his guy, and the meet was pretty much over. They'd have to pin every match to even tie, and that wouldn't happen. By the time it ended, we had defeated them by the biggest margin anyone remembered between our two schools.

117

After our showers, we dressed and headed back out through the gym to grab that dummy and meet with the Rents. Marty and I had permission to ride home with them rather than take the bus. We looked all over for that dummy, and it was gone. Damn! Dad took my bag and told me to head back to the bus for our quickie team get-together that we always had after a meet. Usually it consisted of a reminder of practice times the next day and who our next opponent would be. We always had a little quick celebration when we won, and then we could leave. Coach kept it fun.

Nobody said anything about the dummy on the way home. I felt a little bummed because I wanted it, but I didn't say anything about it—no big deal, really. When we pulled into the garage, Dad said, "Get your gear out of the trunk. Mom needs to get that smelly stuff washed. Hope you showered at school."

"Yeah, yeah," I grumbled under my breath so he wouldn't hear me. When I opened the trunk, all I could say was, "Whoa!"

Dad laughed at me. The dummy with the X'ed out eyes, my picture stapled to the chest, and big J.W. right below lay there in all its glory. Dad and Jim Dad had snagged the fool thing when they left and tossed it into our trunk. Jim Dad and Marty came over from their garage since they got home at the same time that we did to check it out. Mom and Mom Sara went into the house shaking their heads over the male antics of the family. We whooped it up big time as we dragged it into the house while the moms fixed us a snack.

With Christmas right around the corner, I still didn't know what to do yet. I really didn't have any money. Marty and I were in the same boat, more or less. He had money but he had no idea what to get for Jim and Sara. He wanted to do something nice and special, but he had no idea what.

"You know," Marty said. It doesn't matter what I get them, there is no way I could even begin to pay them back for everything they've done for me. Neither one of them care all that much about material stuff so getting them some 'thing' just isn't the answer. It has to be something from the heart."

"I know," I said. "My parents are the same way. They have enough money between both their jobs that if they really want something, they just go out and buy it. Mom says she wants baby stuff. Well, that's all fine and dandy. They can buy whatever they need for the baby. There is no way in hell that I'm going to buy a diaper pail or receiving blanket for Mom for Christmas."

"I know what you mean. I'll buy them both some little things that are relatively inexpensive, but I want something special too. So where's Scott when we need him? He's always good for an idea or two, even if they are bad," Marty grumbled.

119

"Hey! Mind your tongue before I have Mooshy grab it with his fangs, rip it out of your head, and swallow it. It just so happens that I do have an idea, and, like always, it's a good one," Scott said coming out of nowhere. I hadn't even noticed him.

Cracking up, I repeated his words to Marty who immediately turned red all embarrassed.

"I'm sorry, Scott," he said. "I didn't know you were there."

Scott just laughed and told him, "Forget it. I'm kidding. By the way, Guys. Congrats on the way you kicked their butts tonight. How cool was that flying tackle Tommy threw! I almost missed it. Had to wait for Mooshy to finish his dinner before I could come. Got there just in time. Didn't check in with you then 'cause I wanted you concentrating on your matches.

"And, yes, by the way. I do have a Christmas idea for the Rents. Get on your computers and write a separate contract out to each of your parents offering your services for 10-20 hours, whatever you decide, over the course of the next year where you agree to do anything they ask without complaining or whining. You'll scrub floors, wash windows, paint nurseries, weed gardens, clean out eave troughs, wax the car, change a crappy diaper, whatever it takes for those guaranteed hours.

"Make a check off box for each hour of work that they can initial after a particular job's done. After the hours are up, then you can go back to your normal, whiny, procrastinating selves so they will realize what a great deal they had for a Christmas gift. You know, a couple of hours a day between now and when school starts up again in January could almost clear the slate."

Marty and I looked at each other and smiled. Problem solved. We would give each parent fifteen hours of total slavery to do their bidding, whatever it happened to be—providing no diapers were involved. We didn't really want to spend our entire second week of vacation working because we still had practice, but we could knock off some of the hours, that's for sure.

Christmas morning turned into a lark. Just for fun, I did get Mom a diaper pail with some baby butt wipes stuffed inside of it. Everyone enjoyed the hypocrisy of the thing because of my hatred for poopy diapers. While I was at it, I threw a big soft Teddy Bear in the pail too 'cause I wanted to buy the baby a toy. Naturally I had gotten Mom something kind of nice too. I told Jamie about my predicament and she suggested a maternity night gown and robe to keep her warm for the rest of the winter. I told her I'd be too embarrassed to go into one of those kinds of stores by myself.

Realizing that I had no clue as to what I would be doing, she offered to go with me and give me a hand. While we were at it, we picked up an electric razor for Dad. The one he used from the Victorian age was on its last legs. Of course smart alec Marty had to actually go out and spend some real cash while he was at it too.

121

He bought Sara birthstone earrings that made her cry. He bought Jim a watch to replace the one he had broken recently.

Surprisingly, the Rents acted pretty excited about the contracts. Mom started making plans immediately on how to put me to work on them. Her first project involved my painting the nursery between Christmas and new Years. I just smiled and told her I'd get started the next day.

The Rents surprised Marty and me with identical gifts, laptops that we could use for the rest of the year in high school and the next few years in college. We both planned to go to State in the fall and they required laptops. Of course, there were the normal clothes, and I'm sure Dad's idea of a joke, after shave lotion. I hadn't realized how much I had grown recently. Most of my pants were high waters. Finally, a real live growth spurt?

We had Christmas dinner at the Adam's and one of the Rent's brainstorms turned into a discussion about how they could somehow twist hour fifteen into an extension of another five to ten hours. Marty and I spent a lot of time looking at each other and rolling our eyes. What the hell had Scott gotten us into this time? Somewhere out there, I'm sure he was laughing his butt off. Oh well, he could laugh all he wanted. I had a dilemma and needed to put him to work.

Chapter 11

By the time school started back up in January, I had already knocked off seven hours for Mom by painting the nursery and three for Dad. Ever try cleaning the garage with the temperature hovering in the teens? Our first Saturday morning after vacation arrived with no weekend tournament, and it seemed good to sleep in until nine. That's when I started hearing the flack again about sleeping my life away and all that crap. I crawled out of bed, did my morning thing—still couldn't find any whiskers, and headed for breakfast. While I munched on cereal, my cell phone chimed with a text message. It was Sean. "Meet me at the food court in one hour alone."

Now what? Marty had to babysit that morning because Ginny planned to work a half day so that didn't create a problem. I didn't have any other plans so I just glanced at the sports section of the paper while killing forty-five minutes and then headed for the mall.

Sean sat there slurping a cup of coffee with a funny expression on his face when I found him in the corner of the food court with nobody else around him. "Want anything to eat?" he asked when I sat down.

"No, thanks. I was eating breakfast when your message came in. What's up?"

"Two things, actually. First off, Ginny, Bobby, and I went to the cemetery yesterday to visit her husband. I'd never been there before, so it seemed kind of like a thing I should do. While we were there, Bobby moved over to this other grave close by and started mumbling to himself and kind of staring off into space. That's when Ginny told me that it was Scott's grave. I knew it was nearby, but I didn't realize it was that close. Anyway, she told me that Bobby has an imaginary friend over there that he talks to. She said he used to pretend he was talking to Scott, but then later he started telling her it was just a pretend friend. Naturally I had to play dumb about the whole Scott-Bobby thing."

"I wonder if Scott happened to be there?" I said. "I didn't think he spent a whole lot of time out at the cemetery anymore since he moved on to his final dimension. I thought that the only time he comes around now is if I call him. Maybe I should check with him and find out what's going on."

"I was kind of hoping you'd do that. Also, I'm wondering if her husband knows about Ginny and me and what he thinks of it. Of course, we don't know if Scott and her husband have ever come into contact either."

"Ok, I'll do it. You said there were a couple of things that were on your mind. What's the other?"

"One of our officers thought he saw Bruno yesterday out of the corner of his eye. He was headed north on Main Street when an old, beat up pickup passed him traveling south. The guy seemed to just turn his head and stare at him as they crossed paths. By the time it registered with him that it looked like Bruno, and he could get his car turned around and backtrack, the vehicle had disappeared. He told me about it because he knew that Bruno's escape from the mental institution is considered my case."

"Don't like the sounds of that," I said.

"Well, I don't either. I just don't know how much if anything I should tell Marty. If it's a false alarm, there's no sense shaking him up. If there is a problem, then he should be cautioned to be on the alert."

"Let me touch base with Scottie and see if he knows anything on either issue. Give me a day or so and I'll get back with you."

We gabbed another fifteen minutes or so and then he headed out. Ginny left work in an hour so he wanted to go over and

125

relieve Marty and pay him off for the morning before she came home. He kind of liked to help out that way. Ashley was probably over there anyway so they would be glad to have Sean come in and take over their chores. I'm sure they figured they had better things to do.

After I climbed into my car out in the parking lot, I sat back in my seat, shut my eyes, and starting mouthing Scott's name in my head. In no time Scott and Mooshy appeared. Mooshy stood in the back seat slurping on my right ear, and Scott sat in the passenger seat beside me.

"What's up, Dude?" Scott asked in that smart aleck way he had.

"Couple of things. First off, were you out to the cemetery yesterday afternoon when Sean and Ginny were there?"

"Yep! Me and Bobby had a chance to catch up while they were over visiting his dad. Sounds like things might be getting a little serious between those two. According to Bobby he's over there all the time now. Bobby really likes him. He doesn't remember his father so Sean kind of fills that role nicely."

"Sean thought you might be," I told him. "I guess that when Bobby sees you now, he just tells his mom that you're his make-believe friend."

"Yeah, I suggested that one. That way she won't think something's wrong with him. She'd never understand his talking to me. That's also why we talk telepathically all the time now as well. However, sometimes he slips and moves his lips. I had to remind him about that yesterday. I saw Sean watching him."

"Anyway, Sean wants to know if you've ever talked to Ginny's husband, and if he's aware of him He also wants to know what he thinks about their relationship," I said.

"Yeah, he's aware, and he's all for it. He wants Ginny to move on with her life and be happy. He told me to tell you about it earlier, but something came up and then I kinda forgot about it. He died four years ago, and he thinks she's mourned long enough. She's still young and has a long life ahead of her. He likes what he sees in Sean, and thinks he would be a great dad for his boy and husband for his wife."

"I can tell that to Sean than and be honest about the whole thing?"

"Sure," Scott answered. "You said there were a couple of things on your mind. What else?"

"Sean said that there could have been a possible Bruno sighting on Main Street yesterday. One of the officers swore he saw him as they passed. However, by the time he turned the car

127

around, the pickup was long gone. He checked the entire area but couldn't find it. It was kind of like it just disappeared in thin air."

"That wouldn't be good. We don't need that idiot hanging around causing trouble. Marty's just now starting to enjoy life for the first time since him mom died. He sure doesn't need to have Bruno show up on the scene."

"I know. That's what I thought. Sean didn't know for sure if we should say anything to Marty or not. Hate to burst his bubble if it's a false sighting, yet he should be aware if Bruno's out and about again. I just don't know what to do."

"Maybe you should clue in our Moms and Dads and see what they have to say," Scott suggested.

"I think you're right. I'll let both sets know. You know, there's something else too that I wanted to mention. I'm not sure, but I think maybe some of my sensitivities are strengthening. You were there at the mall the other day when I told Sean that I had a vision right out of the blue that he and Ginny were married and had two more kids. I've been getting other little flashes like that more and more lately. Most of the time I just let them pass unless they have some real meaning like that one did. What I was wondering is, can you contact my grandma any time you want to?"

"Sure, when I'm there all I have to do is bring her into my mind and she'll appear. Why?"

"Ok, then, why don't you bring her up in that feeble mentality of yours sometime soon and tell her that I think my sensitivities are strengthening or expanding, or something. See what she has to say about it. You remember she's the one who told me about it in the first place after she died. I'm curious to know if it's normal, and what I should or should not be doing."

"Ok, I'll be going back this afternoon so I'll contact her and see what she says. However, when it comes to talking about you and using the word 'normal?' Well, sometimes I see that as a problem. "

With that he was gone before I could even swat at him. "Jerk!" I said to myself laughing and shaking my head.

***

When I walked into the house, all four rents sat in our kitchen drinking coffee as they planned their day. Sounded to me like they were scheming to head for the casino that afternoon. That's nice! My dinner would consist of fast food again. Strange how Mom didn't worry about my nutritional needs like she used to. For some reason or the other, she kind of figured that I could handle some of that stuff myself. Weird! Oh, well. Maybe that's what she thought; however, I still liked it much better when she cooked.

"Looks like you're neglecting Marty and me again, aren't you?" I grumbled. "I don't suppose there's a thing in the house to eat either."

"Oh, poor baby!" Mom said in her normal sympathetic way. "Maybe Ashley can come over and warm up a can of soup or something so you guys don't starve while we're gone. Of course, if push came to shove, I don't suppose it's beyond reason that you could stir up something for yourselves."

"Yes it is. We like being nurtured and cared for and not being deserted and neglected continuously like it happens all the time these days," I responded trying to look woeful without laughing.

"Someone hold my hand. I might be feeling faint or something. This pity party is really, really getting to me," Mom groaned.

"Oh, by the way, before I forget it. Need to change the subject for a minute. Then we can get back to my trauma. Sean told me that one of the officers thought he saw Bruno Bashore driving down the street yesterday. He tried to turn the car around and find the guy, but the truck disappeared. Don't know if he's really in the area or not, but Sean wanted you to know of the possibility. The big question is, do we tell Marty?"

"Good question," Dad said. "Jim? Sara? What do you think?"

Everyone hashed out all the pros and cons for about fifteen minutes without any decision actually being made. Suddenly the problem resolved itself when Marty and Ashley burst into the kitchen. Marty looked white as a sheet. "Look at this!" he said. "It sat on the dash board of my car when Ashley and I left the Mercers just now."

We looked at it together. It was a very simple note printed out in block, capitol letters, "I KNOW ALL ABOUT ASHLEY! MAYBE I SHOULD TAKE HER FOR A RIDE!"

"Did you tell Sean?" Dad asked.

"Yes! I took it right back inside and showed him. He told me that some cop might have spotted Bruno in town yesterday driving a pickup truck," he spouted out fast and furiously. "I swear! If he's back, I'm not going to put people I love in danger from that maniac! I'll disappear down the road before I let that happen."

Jim Dad put his arm around him and told him softly, "You aren't putting anyone in danger, and you aren't going anywhere. We'll deal with the situation just like we always have. I think he's just trying to scare you and shake you up."

"Well, he's doing a pretty good job of it," Marty muttered under his breath.

Ashley didn't say a word. She didn't let go of his hand either. Now what! The countdown to the state tournament would start before we knew it. Marty and I both had a great shot at placing high at states. Everyone felt especially excited because the state chose our school to host the district tournament, the first leg of the countdown to the states. We really needed the distraction of Bruno back in our lives. Right! Why couldn't that weirdo just disappear permanently?

Everyone instantly forgot the planned trip to the casino that afternoon along with my whining and crying about how neglected Marty and I felt. We had more important things to consider. The two families spent the rest of the afternoon more or less making contingency plans about how we wanted to treat the situation. What it boiled down to, we would continue on with our lives in as normal a fashion as possible, yet keep our eyes and ears wide open to anything out of the ordinary making sure none of us went anywhere alone.

Trying to maintain our normal lives meant meeting the girls at the food court Wednesday evening after practice and dinner. It had sort of become our ritual since none of us had a whole lot of time or money for actual dating with wrestling season in session and nobody having a real job. Oh well, we made the best of the situation. Things had kind of settled down with Lexie. She hadn't done anything questionable or stupid since trying to get me to buy her that hundred and ten dollar pair of jeans so all was well—kind of. Unknown to any of the others, I also met Jamie at the mall almost on a weekly basis as well. Most of the time we would just talk and walk up and down the mall holding hands, killing time, and enjoying each other.

Lexie showed up last Wednesday evening which wasn't all that unusual because she only had to drive in from Holter which was maybe ten miles away. When she walked up to us, she looked really sharp. She had a new top and jeans on.

"Lexie," Ashley asked practically before the, 'Hi's' were all in, "Isn't that the same pair of jeans you were eyeing a couple of weeks ago that are so expensive?"

"Yeah! They look good, don't they? Fit perfectly."

"Where on earth did you get the money for them? Those are designer jeans and pricy as hell."

"Hey! If a person wants something bad enough, there are always ways," she said with a little smirk on her face.

"Lexie, did you steal those jeans?" Ashley asked her point plank.

"I hope you aren't accusing me of being a thief," Lexie snarled as she totally over reacted.

"Hey, I just asked how you happened to have them. Don't get your nose all out of joint."

"Somebody bought them for me. Does that satisfy your curiosity? Come on, Jeremy, let's go for a walk," she said as she grabbed my hand and practically jerked me out of the chair.

She still seemed pretty upset as we walked down the mall. "Jeremy, you don't think I stole these, do you?"

"No! If you say someone bought them for you, I'm cool with that," I told her as we walked along with her head leaning on my shoulder.

"When is this stupid wrestling season going to be over so we can actually have some time together? You know, I would actually like for the two of us to go to the gravel pit again just so I can prove to you that I really am a lady and can act like one."

"Oh, we will," I assured her. "Season's really just getting started, but it goes quickly. I'll have lots of time then."

"Let's go in here. I want to look around," she interrupted as we walked past the mall's video store.

"What are you looking for in here? Anything in particular?" I asked.

"No, not really. Just want to see what's new out on Blue Ray."

We kind of separated in the store. I checked out the music CDs while she looked at the movies. The Red Hot Chile Peppers just released a new album and I wasn't even aware of it. I looked over at Lexie to tell her just as she slipped a movie into her purse.

I went right over to her and asked, "Lexie, what're you doing putting that movie in your purse?"

"Are you going to buy it for me?" she asked with a big grin on her face.

"Hell no, and you aren't going to steal it either! Put it back!" I demanded.

"Oh, Jeremy, chill! I was just teasing. I saw you watching me, so I just thought it would be funny because of what happened earlier," she said as she returned the Blue Ray DVD to the rack.

"Let's go back and find Ashley and Marty," I said. I have a ton of homework tonight and have to get busy.

We both knew that I intentionally cut the night short, but, oh well, tough! I wanted to digest the day's events a little. Maybe I'd call in Scott and see what he had to say. Right! I already knew exactly what he would say. Why bother?

135

However, lo and behold, who should show up at the foot of my bed that night while I tossed and turned and beat myself up mentally?

"Get it through your head, Bro!" Scott yelled while Mooshy curled up and squinted at me out of one eye wondering why Scottie was yelling at me this time. "She's hard core. She's a thief! She's a lying bitch! How much more proof do you need? She's not your type. What are you going to do if she steals something when she's with you and gets caught? Then you're an accomplice. If you've got a record, you aren't going to get into State next year. Forget it! Then you will end up with that job we talked about before with you riding at the back end of the garbage truck—provided, that is, if you can get someone to actually hire you. In this economy people are fussy who they employ these days. If you don't end up in jail you'll end up living with your parents for the rest of your life!" Scott ranted on and on.

"Scott!" I finally yelled back telepathically so that the Rents wouldn't hear. "Would you please just shut up a minute and listen! You're right! I know you're right, and I'm gonna do it. I just need that right excuse and I'll do it. Don't worry! I'm not gonna let her get me into any trouble."

Things eventually cooled down, we talked normally, and Mooshy quit glaring at me and went back to sleep. We agreed that I didn't want to hurt Ashley's feelings by letting her know what her cousin was really a tramp, but I'd had enough. The time

136

had come to break the relationship off. Besides, maybe it was time to pursue Jamie a little bit more just to see how that might work out.

Just before he left, Scott said, "Oh, by the way, before I forget, I talked to your grandma the other night about your powers and all that. She said that as long as you don't intentionally try to inhibit them, they more than likely will continue to develop stronger and stronger as you get older. Sometimes they will even branch out to other areas sort of like they did when you saw Sean and Ginny married in the future with two more kids besides Bobby."

"Yeah, but suppose I start to develop powers that I don't want?" I asked. "For instance, I wouldn't want to know that somebody was going to croak."

"I don't know," he said. "Maybe if you start getting those kinds of flashes in the future you'll just have to figure out how to block them. Your grandma didn't seem to think it was any big deal anyway. Also, just for the record, she didn't say one thing about you being 'normal' either."

Dear Scott—with him, some things would never change. After he left, I started worrying about how much control I would have over my own powers. I liked being able to see and communicate with Scott, but I didn't know if I wanted to be aware of all the ghosts that are out and about. Also I didn't want to start developing other powers that I couldn't control. For instance, getting fun flashes in the future like Bobby harassing Sean was fine, I just wouldn't want to get a flash of one of my loved ones dying.

Fortunately, for the immediate future, anyway, the flashes kind of took a breather and none too soon. The wrestling season started winding down and tournament row approached. Needless to say, nothing ever goes right. I turned into a nervous wreck and not just because of the tournament.

Chapter 12

The long, cold, harsh winter dragged on and on as always. Fortunately, a lot was going on to help keep my mind off the weather. For one thing, we had a big wrestling tournament almost every Saturday. On the last Saturday in January, Holter held the last regular tournament of the season. We skipped one week, and then came the county league meet, which Marty and I both won, followed in a row by districts, regionals, and states.

We held the district tournament that year. Many of the schools didn't have the facilities, organization, or desire to handle a tournament of that magnitude. Ours did. Therefore, our school typically hosted either the district tournament or the regional tournament every couple of years. One of the major state universities almost always held the state tournament.

The first of the sixteen visiting team busses pulled in about seven o'clock Saturday morning. They had to do a lot of things before the first match started at eleven. Weighing in and feeding breakfast to one hundred and ninety-two wrestlers plus all the coaches took a lot of time and organization.

The wrestling club always handled the tournaments so everything ran smoothly. The wrestler's fathers worked the scoring tables, the mothers worked in the kitchen, and brothers and sisters cleaned up the cafeteria and ran bout cards from the mats to the head table. As always, manning the tournaments was a family affair. Even Ashley helped out cleaning tables and working in the kitchen. Lexie couldn't be bothered. Her energies were used up ogling the cute guys and acting bored out of her mind.

When we finally hit the mats for the first time, I won my match by a decision, and Marty pinned his opponent in the first period. Our second match of the day came an hour and a half hour later with pretty much the same results. We won meaning we had down time until the finals started at six.

Out in the hall Jim Dad found Dad looking at the charts. "What say we run down to the Guillotine for a quick burger and beer while we're killing time? The wives are all tied up in the kitchen and will never miss us."

"Sounds good to me," Dad answered. "I want to go find Tom Moore. He and I have been hashing over a project at work so the break will do us all good. I'll meet you right back here in just a second. He's sitting out there with Ashley and Alexis and looks a little bored, to say the least. He doesn't know squat about wrestling, but he really likes Marty and came out today just to support him."

"He must be ready for that break then," Jim Dad smiled.

After rounding up everyone in their little group, they headed for the Guillotine—a restaurant-bar combination downtown, that catered to all of the local sports enthusiasts. They had large pictures of all the state champions of the past few years on the wall. They accommodated the wrestling crowd more than anyone else since the owner, Bob McCally, more commonly known as Big Mac, was a former heavyweight wrestling champion and one of the town's biggest financial supporters of the wrestling team. What a difference between him and Bruno Bashore. Both were ex heavyweight wrestling champions, and polar opposites in personality. Mac was a gentle giant if there ever was such a thing.

Apparently, Mr. McCally got all excited when he saw their little group walk in. He knew that we'd made the finals since we obviously weren't wrestling in the consolation rounds or they wouldn't have been there.

When they sat down, Bob plopped a big bowl of popcorn down on the table wanting all the details. McCally always made saltiest popcorn anyone's ever tasted. The rumor had it that the salt mines in Detroit would go out of business if he ever stopped his popcorn routine. Besides, it was great for business. That popcorn was good for at least two extra pitchers of whatever the customers drank.

＊＊

Sneaking in the back door, the long lost group headed straight to the cafeteria. The final semi-consolation round had just finished so the crowd had nothing better to do but hang around and wait for the championships. Marty and I plus the girls sat together on the stage with our feet dangling over the edge talking and drinking a diet soft drink watching.

"Hi, Dad," I spoke when they got close. "Where have you guys been all afternoon? Mom and Mom Sara have been having a fit."

"They're just mad because we didn't invite them. Besides, we had things to do. We've been down to the Guillotine planning our big victory celebration for tonight when you guys win your district championships."

"Sounds like fun. This isn't going to be one of those 'parents only' shindigs is it? We want to go too," I said.

"No sweat!" said Jim Dad. "This is for families. Everyone gets in on this celebration. Mr. McCally invited all of our winners and their families. Going to be tons of soft drinks and snacks.

"Good! Guess we'd better win tonight so we can go too," Marty said looking at me with a grin.

"Actually, it was all Mac's idea. He suggested we should throw a big party there tonight for all the kids and parents going on to regionals. He would set up a special champion's table for all of our guys. He promised to load up the tables with pitchers of soft drinks, pretzels, popcorn, and stuff like that. He said if anyone wanted to order food, that'd be fine too. It didn't matter. He just wanted to celebrate.

"Then I asked him what time we had to have the kids out since it's technically a bar, but Mac told us not to worry. He'd just seat everyone in the banquet room upstairs so it would be a private party. They won't serve anyone alcohol in the room. If any of the adults want a drink, they'll have to go downstairs to the bar.

"So, with that settled, we spent the rest of the afternoon eating that infernal popcorn and quenching the salt from our palates before we had to come back for finals. Love that raspberry iced tea."

"Yeah, right!" I answered sarcastically.

During the break Alexis figured she'd had enough. She wanted to go home. Ashley acted a little disappointed, but that was fine by me. All she'd done all day was to complain about how boring it was. I think the only thing she enjoyed was watching the wrestlers run around in their uniforms that showed off their bods. I think she thought that she was making me jealous. Little did she know I would have loved it if she had hooked up with some other dude.

There is nothing funnier than watching some mother or father when their son is in the middle of a match. They go though more deformed body gyrations than most professional contortionists. Dad and Jim Dad were no exceptions. It always made the spectators laugh because they did it right there in full view of everyone in the place.

By the time I set up the stack move in my championship match, Dad had slipped down to the edge of the mat with Coach. When I cranked it up, Dad literally had his head balanced on the mat mirroring mine much to the delight of the people watching him. With the kid's shoulders flat on the mat, and his feet flapping in the air, the ref slapped the mat. The district championship was mine.

I jumped to my feet and cut loose with a war whoop!

Getting ready for the awards ceremony, the tournament director handed Dad the medals. It was customary at our school that whenever a local boy won a tournament, one or both of his parents had the honor of presenting the medals to him at the awards ceremony. It always seemed like a nice touch.

As the announcer named the winners, Dad handed each of us our medal and shook our hands. Mom gave each of us a little kiss on the cheek along with her congratulations. I turned crimson and the other two guys laughed at me. Oh, well!

Marty's match followed mine. He went out on the mat and took control of the match right from the start. He double-legged the guy within the first twenty seconds. By the time another twenty seconds passed, he slipped in a half nelson, turned the kid on his back, and flattened his shoulders to the mat for the pin. Jim Dad and Mom Sara presented Marty's medal to his group.

By the time the district tournament finished, our school had chalked up three firsts, one second, and four thirds. It had been a great day. Time to party at the Guillotine!

When our clan finally left the school around ten, snow had started to fall. It was a beautiful night. The lights of the parking lot made the falling snow sparkle and everyone appeared happy.

About fifty people altogether converged at the banquet room at the Guillotine. Dad and Jim Dad spread the word to all of the families of kids who had advanced on to the regional, and most of them came. Bob McCally even moved the band from the main area upstairs to the banquet room.

145

The long, loud, and boisterous celebration lasted for a couple of hours. Sounded like a bunch of drunks in there with everyone trying to out-shout and yell each other.

My steak dinner tasted great! Few of the wrestlers had eaten what you'd call a decent meal in the three months since wrestling started back in November. All of them enjoyed themselves tremendously.

By eleven thirty some of the people started to leave. The storm had turned into a blizzard and the snow kept piling up heavier and heavier. People started getting a bit edgy about that. Also, the wrestlers themselves were exhausted. It had been a long day for everyone.

"Mom," I asked about midnight. "Can we go home now? Dad has his own car here so we don't have to wait for him. He and Mr. Moore have been talking shop all day about some project they are working on and they're still going at it. They are even talking about going over to the office tonight. Why don't we go? I'm tired!"

"Okay. I'll tell your dad that we're leaving."

When Mom, Mom Sara, Jim Dad, Marty, Ashley and I all started to put on our coats, it kind of acted like a catalyst for everyone else to do the same. Everyone except Dad and Tom Moore, they stayed behind with their coffee cups being refilled

146

every five minutes. They continued to talk about that big project from work. Mrs. Moore, Ashley's mom, drove by herself so the two of them took off leaving the dads to their workaholic selves.

Before we left, Mom and I went over and thanked Mr. McCally for the party. The night had been a great sendoff for the regional tournament to be held the following week.

"Drive carefully, everybody," Dad called out as we headed out to the parking lot to go to our cars. "Looks like the snow's really starting to pile up."

"We will," Mom told him. "You do the same. If you and Tom do go to the office, don't stay long!"

By the time we made it home and put the car in the garage, the wind had started to pick up even stronger.

"Boy, what a miserable night this turned out to be," Mom mentioned to me as she hung her coat in the closet. "If this wind keeps up, you kids sure won't have to worry about school Monday morning."

"Right! You know how that goes," I laughed. "By tomorrow morning the snow will be finished and they'll be out plowing the streets. By the afternoon you'll never be able to tell that we had a blizzard. No snow day this time."

147

We sat down to talk and unwind a bit before heading off to bed. While we rehashed the day, we heard what sounded like a huge explosion way off in the distance. Sounded pretty eerie through the snow and howling wind. Shortly afterwards we could hear the mournful wail of a number of sirens.

"Oh boy, there goes the ambulance. You can tell by its siren. This is sure no night for somebody to have an accident or be sick. It would take forever to get to the hospital in this," Mom commented as the emergency vehicle crept past the corner down on the main drag.

"I don't know," I answered with an ear still on all the sirens. "There must be something serious going on. I hope that nobody going home from the tournament or from the party had any serious problems. I wonder if it has anything to do with that big boom we heard. Hopefully two cars didn't come together and blow up or something."

Mom and I sat up for another hour talking about the day's events. It had been a great day. Next week we would all go through the same thing again at the regional at the southern end of the state. More than likely, everyone would go down Friday night when the team did and stay in motels for the weekend.

Mom and I were just about ready to give up on Dad and go to bed when a car pulled into the driveway. Thinking that he finally got home made us both feel better. That is until the door bell

148

rang. I bolted to the door and opened it. There stood Sean O'Connor.

"Sean, come on in," I said. "What's going on? It's terrible out there."

By then Mom was at my side also wondering why he'd showed up when he did.

"There's been an explosion at your dad's office building. Mr. Moore let him off at the door while he parked the car. When Mr. Wright unlocked the door and turned on the lights, the place blew up. The explosion threw him about thirty feet out into the yard. He's at the hospital in the emergency room and appears to be hurt badly. Grab your coats and I will take you. I don't want either one of you driving in this storm."

Mom and I were out the door in less than a minute. In route I dug out my cell phone and called Jim Dad. I apologized for getting them out of bed, but I knew they'd want to know. Jim said they would meet us at the hospital as soon as they could get dressed and get there. Things didn't sound good.

Chapter 13

Sean's car crawled down the road. The heavy, blinding snow literally swirled with the forty miles an hour winds. I only saw one or two other cars. Good thing! Nobody talked a whole lot as we headed to the hospital. Sean concentrated on his driving while Mom and I lost ourselves in own thoughts. Thank God Sean drove us to the hospital. By the time we got there, I was a basket case. If I'd driven, we'd probably ended up wrapped around some tree.

The three of us hustled into the emergency room. Sean went up to the triage desk and told her. "Ted Wright."

"Back in room three," she motioned with her thumb as she pushed the button to open the door.

When we walked into the room, Dad lay on the bed with his eyes shut. "He hasn't awakened yet," Tom told us. He'd followed the ambulance to the hospital and stayed with Dad until we arrived.

"So, what happened?" Mom asked.

"Not really sure. Because of the blizzard, we didn't bother driving both cars. I have four-wheel drive on my truck so we left his at the Guillotine. When we finally made it there, I drove right up to the front door and dropped him off so he could get out of the snow and open up while I backed up to park in the lot. I didn't want to block the front of the door. Don't really know why, force of habit I guess—lucky too.

"That's when it happened. I saw the lights go on, and then a huge fireball. Ted flew probably thirty feet through the air and landed on his back. The blast actually cracked the windshield on my SUV in several places. Fortunately, I keep a blanket behind the seat. I draped it over him being careful not to move him in any way. By the time I pulled my cell phone out and called 911, I could already hear the emergency crews on the way."

"Has he been out all this time?" I asked.

"He hasn't moved since I reached him there in the snow," Tom answered. "The doctor who initially checked him out said that nothing appears to be broken, but they won't know for sure until they x-ray him and do a CT scan. I think they're getting ready to do that now."

Shortly thereafter a couple of orderlies came and carted him away. They told us to wait there in his cubicle, and they would bring him right back. While he was in radiology, Mom Sara, Jim Dad, and Marty all flew in the door. The orderlies were probably gone for a half hour before they wheeled him back. Naturally, they had no clue as to the extent of his injuries. If they did, they weren't saying. It seemed forever before the doctor finally came back. We all just sat around talking, wondering what had happened while we waited. Since we had a ride home, Sean decided to leave. He said he wanted to go back out to the scene and poke around.

Finally, the doctor came into the room. "We did a full body CT scan and X-rays on Mr. Wright. The X-ray shows no broken bones, and the scan shows no internal injuries to any of the organs. However, he does appear to have a severe concussion and is comatose. There is major swelling on the brain. The good news is there doesn't appear to be any bleeding going on which could cause very serious problems. Now, when he wakes up, expect him to have a severe headache, and he'll probably be nauseous. Don't know when that'll be, but we're going to keep him for a day or two anyway. I have already signed admittance papers. They're getting his room ready now."

We all followed Dad up to his room. After a while Mom told me, "Jeremy, I want you to go home and get some sleep. I'm going to spend the rest of the night with Dad."

"But, Mom! I want to stay," I complained.

152

"No buts. It's very late, and you're exhausted and need to get some sleep. I'll be fine," she said digging out the keys to his car and giving them to me.

"Ok, but I'll be back in the morning."

"That's fine. In the meantime, scat!" she said as she gave me a hug and smile. That fake smile didn't convince me or anyone else.

I Rode with Jim Dad, Mom Sara, and Marty. They took me to the Guillotine to pick up Dad's car. Marty rode with me while Jim and Sara followed.

It took a lot longer to get home that night than normal. Even though it had quit snowing, the wind howled and blew a good six inches of the stuff all over the place making it really slippery. Marty and I didn't talk much. We were both too busy watching the road for drifts and icy spots. It sure seemed good when we pulled into the garage.

Marty didn't even bother to come in. He was dog-tired as well and headed right for his house. He said he intended to go straight to bed—in other words, don't call. Our house was pitch dark and creepily quiet when I walked in. I didn't particularly like being home all by myself under the circumstances. Normally I liked it. Oh well, I'd survive. I hung up my coat and turned on the TV. I don't really know why, just for something to do I guess. I sat

153

down on the sofa and flipped through the channels. The only thing vaguely interesting was a Pistons – Lakers replay on ESPN—the actual game had finished hours ago. I watched it for maybe five minutes and said screw it and went to bed. I got to my room, turned on the light, and there sat Scott and Mooshy on my bed.

"Thought maybe you might need a little company," Scott said.

"You have no idea how bad," I said feeling better just having them there.

We talked for just a little while when Scott said, "You can hardly keep your eyes open. Go ahead and get some sleep, and we'll spend the night. I'll be in my bed if you need anything."

Mooshy slept with me. He snuggled up to me, and I held him all night. He always knew which one of us needed him the most at any given time. Every time I woke up or stirred during the night, he raised his head and lapped me across the face. It helped.

I didn't sleep worth a darn all night so I got a lot of laps. My mind kept rehashing about Dad and the explosion. Why did the place blow up? There had to be a reason. Would it have blown up if nobody had opened the door? What would have happened if nobody had gone in until Monday morning? Would somebody have smelled the gas by then and reported it? Did Sean find out anything when he went back? My mind kept spinning round and round going from one question to the next over and over.

About eight o'clock in the morning I gave up and crawled out of bed and headed for the shower. I had kept my cell phone on my night stand just in case Mom called. I wanted to hear from her, but I didn't. The last thing I wanted was for her to call in the middle of the night. That would mean nothing but bad news. I might've slept two hours max. Scott and Mooshy kept me company while I scarfed down something to eat, but then they left saying they were going to the hospital early to check up on dad.

Marty called around nine. "Hey! You hear anything this morning?" he asked.

"No. I'm getting ready to go up to the hospital now. Want to ride along?"

"No. Mom Sara said you should probably go up by yourself this morning so you can talk to your Mom alone. I'll come up later when they go—probably around noon or so."

"Ok. If there is anything really important to report, I'll call you when I get a chance."

The snowplows had cleaned our street during the middle of the night so I had to get the snow blower out and clear out the drive and sidewalk before I could get out. They had filled in the end of the driveway big time. I wasn't particularly in the mood to be messing with tons of snow, but I didn't have a whole lot of choice in the matter if I intended to get out.

When I finally walked into Dad's room, it didn't look like anything had changed from when I'd left. Mom sat in the same chair, and Dad still lay there with his eyes closed. Didn't look like either one of them had budged.

"Hi, Mom," I said when I walked in. "Any doctors or anybody been in this morning?"

"Doctors and nurses have wandered in and out all night. I don't know how many times they've taken his vitals. All I know is his blood pressure, pulse, and temperatures all stayed consistent. Apparently that's a good sign. He just won't wake up."

"Anyone say how long it might be?" I asked.

"Not really. One doctor talked to me about an hour ago and said that they never know in instances like this. He could wake up any minute, or it might take weeks or months. He said that when his body and brain are ready to wake up, they will, and there's nothing anyone can do to speed up the process."

I didn't like the sounds of that one bit.

And then she broke down. The only other time I've ever heard her sob like that was the day that Scott died. I held her and told her everything would be okay. I didn't know what else to do.

"Jeremy, I don't think I could stand to lose your dad, especially now with the baby on the way. We wanted another child when you were younger, but it just never happened."

I didn't know what to say, but the first words out of my mouth were, "I'm still not changing any poopy diapers!"

For some reason or the other, that stupid comment broke the tension and Mom started laughing.

Marty, Jim, and Sara wandered in about twelve-fifteen.

"Any news?" Sara asked immediately as she grabbed Mom and hugged her.

"Nothing. Doctors don't know when he's going to wake up so here I sit until he does."

No way could she pull a continuous vigil like that so we set up a visitation schedule while everyone was there. Mom had to go home and get some sleep. She looked terrible. Jim Dad would stay until six, and then I would relieve him until nine, and then Mom would come back and spend the night. Sara planned to relieve her in the morning.

Marty and I rode home together. We stopped off for a quickie burger en route. He told me that he'd notified Ashley about Dad, and that she would let Lexie know. When we finally got home, he headed into their house, and I went into ours. I checked on Mom and found her in bed sound asleep. Sure hadn't taken her long. I settled down on the corner of the sofa and turned on the TV to one the sports channels. That's the last I remember until about a quarter of six. I guess that I'd crashed big time. I hadn't even heard Mom come into the room. She'd shut off the TV and thrown a blanket over me and left. Probably headed back to the hospital. Damn! She's the one who's supposed to be sleeping!

When I finally showed up at the hospital to relieve Jim and shoo Mom out of there—almost a half hour late, nothing had changed. He said that the doctors and nurses had drifted in and out all day. They kept shifting Dad's position on his bed so he wouldn't get bed sores, and taking his vitals, but that was about the extent of the news. We talked for a little while and then he left dragging her out with him. She was due back in a couple of hours.

After he left, I pulled the chair up to the side of the bed. I started talking to Dad and rubbing his hand. It felt warm. That seemed like a good sign to me, but what did I know. I talked to him about a lot of things the whole time I sat there—wrestling, school, Lexie, what I wanted to do in college next year, where I wanted to go, Marty, Bruno, and anything else I could think of. I just wanted to tell him everything going on and everything on my mind. The next thing I knew, Mom stood behind me rubbing my shoulders.

"Get it all off your chest?" she asked.

"Yeah, I think so," I smiled a bit sheepishly.

"You tell him that you love him?" she asked.

"Of course, a couple of times anyway. You know, the one thing I never managed to tell Scott before he died was how much our near brother relationship meant to me."

"I know. It's one of those things we all just kind of take for granted. Your dad isn't going to die though. I'm pretty sure of that. We just don't know when or if he's going to wake up."

159

Chapter 14

Monday turned into a real bummer at school. I didn't want to be there, but if I intended to wrestle in the regional tournament that weekend, I had to. Marty and Ashley acted great. They tried to keep everything upbeat in school so I wouldn't get too down, because with everything going on, I just couldn't get my head on straight.

Practice went dreadfully bad. I just couldn't get into it. I wouldn't have blamed Marty one bit if he had asked for a different partner. I sucked! I basically just went through the motions. He picked on me continuously trying to get my spirits up. It didn't work. Coach didn't say a word about it.

On Wednesday morning during English class, an office aid came down to our room with a note. They wanted me in the conference room. When I walked in, there sat Mom and Sean. I panicked! Dad had died!

"Calm down!" they both said practically in unison when they saw my reaction. "Nothing has changed with Dad," Mom said. "We just received some other news that we needed to share with you alone."

"Now what?" I sputtered.

"I just talked to the fire marshal. He hasn't totally completed his investigation, but he has come to some conclusions," Sean said as he settled back in his chair. "I've seen the building and how trashed it was from the explosion, so I can imagine the job it must be to figure anything out. However, these guys are very professional and skilled at what they do. Some of the science they do is truly amazing."

"So get to the point! What'd they find?" I demanded sounding a little testier than I would have under normal circumstances. I knew Sean supported me one hundred percent, and I felt bad after I said it. "I'm sorry!" I told him almost immediately. "I didn't mean to spout off."

"Don't sweat it, Jeremy. I totally understand," he said with a smile. "The point is the fire marshal discovered that somebody apparently broke into the back entrance with something like a crowbar. Also, it appears like that person or somebody with him unscrewed the bolt holding the pipe going into the gas meter. In other words, he thinks somebody intentionally caused the explosion."

161

"Bruno?" I asked.

"Not sure. However, I sure wouldn't rule it out at this point. They're looking for prints, but don't know if they'd still be able to find anything after all the heat generated by the blast and fire."

"Oh great! Just what the hell we need right now with Marty and me trying to get ready for the regionals this weekend." I groused.

"We aren't going to tell him," Mom said getting into the conversation for the first time. "I've already talked to Sara and Jim, and we all agreed to let you know so you can keep your eyes open, but not to say anything to Marty at least for the time being."

"The thing is, you need to be extra vigilant. Another thing, do we let Ashley in on this? Lately, if you aren't with him, she is. What do you think?"

"She doesn't even know what Bruno looks like. I think that might be a bit much to put on her shoulders. I'll just make sure I'm with him as much as possible."

"Sounds cool to me," Sean said. "In the mean time, what are you going to tell them when you go back to class?"

"How about if I just say that there was some involuntary movement on Dad's part, and the doctors thought I should be notified just in case he wakes up so it won't be such a big surprise."

"That works for me," Mom said as she stood up and headed for the door and back to the hospital. "In the mean time, keep your eyes open and your cell phone charged," she said as she gave me a little kiss on the forehead.

Sean walked with me back to class. "I don't think Bruno would have the guts to try to harm either one of you out in the open. Just stay alert, pay attention, and don't let yourself get caught by yourself in some deserted area. If you have to, park in the handicap area at school. I'll see if I can get you a temporary permit that you can use. I don't want you at the back of the parking lot for any reason. Also, while I'm at it, take this."

"What is it?" I asked. Looked like a large aerosol mouth spray.

"It's Pepper Spray. It's perfectly legal and is very effective. I have one for Marty too. Now, let me show you how to use it so you don't' screw up and blast yourself with it," he teased.

And he did. He also cautioned me about keeping it out of sight and not to be showing it off to any of my friends around school because of the zero tolerance policy.

163

"Oh, by the way," he cautioned just before he left giving me that arched eyebrow look. "Make darned sure you don't accidentally set that thing off in your pocket. Pepper spray burns the skin on contact and that's a little too close to certain sensitive parts for comfort."

"Ooooo!" I promised to be careful.

Fortunately I didn't have to use the handicap permit that Sean provided. Don't know how I'd explain that one to Marty or anyone else at school. Things remained hectic enough without that being added to the mix. Between going to school, getting ready for the regional tournament, visiting Dad every night at the hospital, the week dragged big time. I just wanted it to be over. I was getting to the point that I didn't care if I won Saturday or not. Wrestling was almost becoming a distraction with everything else going on.

Marty and Ashley were great. They both did everything they could to keep me propped up. Didn't hear much from Lexie. She called a couple of times, but that was about it. During practice Marty kept threatening to bust me in the nose with an elbow just to get my attention. He was joking, of course. That's what Bruno always wanted him to do. We'd laugh and then I would try to get serious. Marty would have a great chance at a state title if his workout partner could only get his act together. I felt guiltier as the week went by. I just couldn't get my head into it.

I seriously considered calling in Scott, but I couldn't. My petty problems were not reason enough to ask him for help. It had to be something serious. He made that very clear the first time that I saw him after he died that he could only be called for something truly serious, not a personal pity party. Besides, I figured his showing up the other night for support was above and beyond the call of duty for him.

I think I received the most unexpected outside support from Jamie in chemistry class. She propped me up big time. Every day she asked about Dad. She wanted to know everything. She especially wanted to know how I was holding up. She couldn't believe that Lexie hadn't even stopped by the hospital when I pulled my shift from seven to nine every evening.

On Wednesday night I hadn't much more than gotten to Dad's room at the hospital when my phone rang. I checked caller ID before answering—Lexie, damn! "Where are you?" she demanded rather indignantly.

"I'm at the hospital. Where'd you think?"

"It's Wednesday night, and you're supposed to be at the mall with me."

"Excuse me? My dad's lying here in a coma in case you forgot. I sit here with him every night from seven to nine relieving my Mom so she can eat dinner and get in a little rest break before she

165

has to come back for the night," I said hardly believing that I had to explain myself.

"Oh, come on, Jeremy! He's in a coma. He doesn't know if you're there or not. I wanted to talk to you tonight. I have something important to tell you. Why don't you just slip out for an hour and nobody will know the difference."

"Lexie, there's something I've been wanting to talk to you about too. I intended to wait until we could be alone together, but it might as well be right now. We have nothing in common. I'm trying to get ready for college, and you think I should go get a job so I can buy you stuff. My family is very important to me, and you could care less. Wrestling and the state tournament coming up are also very important to me, and you're bored out of your skull. None of this has even remotely worked out between us. We have entirely different values and interests. I just don't see any reason for us to see each other anymore. I'm sorry."

"Gee, Jeremy, for probably the first time ever I guess we're really on the same wave length after all. That's why I wanted to meet with you so badly tonight at the mall. I know that Marty and Ashley aren't going to be there so that's why I wanted to see you alone. I planned to break up with you tonight, but damn, you beat me to the punch. I've found someone new."

"Hey! I'm happy for you. Somebody from your school?"

"Yeah. This new guy is super cool. I've been dating him for a couple of weeks now, and he likes to do all kinds of things outside of school. He really likes to party. He used to play basketball, but he's been out of it for a year so he can't play this year. Besides, the season is almost over so it doesn't matter anyway. He told me that there had been a problem with his old girl friend at his previous school and so he had spent the past year going to some idiotic military academy. We've really hit it off big. The only thing I don't like is his name. Can you imagine anyone ever calling their kid, Moose?"

I popped the biggest shit-eating grin you've ever seen, "Really!" I said. "Well, it sounds like you and your friend Moose are made for each other. I can only wish the two of you the best. Give Mortimer my regards."

"Who? What are you talking about? Who's Mortimer?"

"Nothing! Nothing! Forget it! Just thinking out loud. Anyway, you and Moose have a great time. I must say our time together has been interesting, if nothing else. Bye! I've got to go," and I hung up the phone laughing.

That put me in a good mood all day Thursday. I told Marty the whole story in English class. He and Ashley had pretty much figured out the deal with Lexie but had always hoped for the best. Some of what I told him—like the trip back to the pit the first night we went there as a group, completely surprised him. He

167

couldn't wait to fill in Ashley on the latest any more than I could to tell Jamie.

I unloaded on Jamie that afternoon in the chemistry lab. She couldn't believe her ears. I had told her a lot of it before, but not everything. This time I held nothing back. I told her everything— getting things off my chest while she listened and did the experiment we were supposed to be doing together. She even did the paper work which I normally did when we shared responsibilities. Just before the end of the hour, she took my hand in hers and told me how sorry she was about everything I had gone through. I almost melted right there on the spot.

That night about seven fifteen, I sat in the chair beside Dad's bed and told him about the girl in my chemistry class that really interested me. Suddenly, someone started massaging the back of my neck and shoulders. I thought that Mom had come back early. I turned around and there stood Jamie.

"Well, hi!" I said totally surprised to see her there. "Here, grab this seat while I pull another one over. Can you stay a little while?"

"You know, there's just something about you sitting up here every night all alone with just you and your dad that bothered me. I have a commitment tomorrow night and can't come then, but I had nothing to do tonight so I thought I'd just come up and sit with you if that's okay. I know you spend this time talking to your dad so feel free. I'm not going to take that away from you just because I'm here. You don't have to talk to me, just know that I care, and I'm here for you."

"You don't think it's weird talking to someone who's in a coma?" I asked. "Lexie said that it was completely stupid. I might as well be talking to the wall."

"Jeremy, there's nothing weird or stupid about it at all. I've heard that sometimes people in comas not only hear what is being said, but they also remember. So, don't you think you should introduce us?" she asked.

"Yeah, I'd really like that. Dad, I want you to meet my friend, Jamie. Jamie, this is my dad," I said not feeling at all dim-witted like I would have if it had been Lexie.

"Hi, Mr. Wright. Glad to meet you. Hope you remember that we've already met when you wake up. If you don't, that's ok too. We'll just make Jeremy introduce us again," she said with a smile as she scrunched up her nose at me. I laughed. "Jeremy and I have known each other since the seventh grade. We've shared a ton of classes together and have always been friends."

While she talked to Dad, I looked at her totally amazed. She took my hand in hers and we sat there holding hands. It felt so natural. I guess I hadn't ever really looked at her before. She had naturally blond hair with a slight wave in it. Might be a little

169

darker than what it had been in the seventh grade when I first met her. I remember thinking at the time that she must have bleached it. The blemish free, creamy, soft skin on her face looked perfect. Her eyes were a very striking blue color, not dark and not washed out, but just a nice in-between. I liked them. I liked her.

After we told Dad about our personal history in school together, I finished telling him about my day. I explained what had gone on in practice and how Marty had threatened to bust me in the nose again for the fourth time that week. I let him know that I really had to get my act together. Every once in a while Jamie would add something or the other to the conversation. We both pretty much talked to him and not to each other. I don't remember what had been said, but we were both laughing when Mom walked in.

"Hi, Honey!" she said as she took off her coat and hung it up. She looked absolutely exhausted. At least she hadn't been staying all night the past few days. She'd stay until about eleven and then come home and try to get some sleep. I'm sure she thought that Jamie was Lexie when she walked in. So I introduced them immediately. Lexie had never actually talked to either one of my parents. That didn't interest her one bit. Socializing with the old folks was totally un-cool in her eyes. Mom acted like absolutely nothing had gone on out of the ordinary, which amazed me because I hadn't thought to tell her earlier that Lexie and I broke up.

After Mom took over the shift, Jamie and I went down to the cafeteria and put away a coke and a brownie and talked for a few more minutes before leaving to go home.

I intended to stay up and tell Mom all about the Lexie breakup and Jamie when she came home around eleven twenty. However, I fell sound asleep on the sofa again so she threw a blanket over me and went to bed herself. That's ok, I needed the rest. Little did I know right then, but not too long after that, Jamie's parents were going to decide they wanted to meet me. According to her, her dad was a real piece of work. Oh, joy!

Chapter 15

Jamie and I managed to see each other a couple of times in the next week. We went to a movie on Sunday night after my hospital gig, and then met at the mall on Tuesday after practice. Marty and Ashley were there too and the four of us had a really good time. Most of the time we spent at the food court laughing over a coke that we nursed for an hour. Before we left to go home, we walked a couple of laps around the mall held hands and just talked. Everything we did just felt so unforced and perfectly natural. Jamie and I seemed like a good fit. I was falling for her.

We were on our second lap and neither of us had said anything for a minute or two when Jamie said, "Okay, Jeremy, you ready for a zinger?" she asked.

"Sure, what gives?" I asked suddenly worried that maybe she wanted to break up with me or something. I get paranoid easily at times.

"Mom and Dad want to meet you so Mom's invited you to come to dinner tomorrow night. We normally eat about five thirty. If you get there at five you'll have plenty of time to meet them, eat, and then get to the hospital at seven."

"You act kinda leery. What's the matter? Doesn't sound like you're too enthused about the idea."

"It's my dad," she answered. "He can be kind of a jerk when he wants to be. He's made up his mind that he doesn't like you even though he's never even seen you."

"Why? What does he think I've done that's so terrible?" I asked really wondering why. I thought I was a fairly decent person.

"Part of it is because you're a boy and I'm his baby girl. Excuse me a minute while I barf!" she laughed before going on. "He's always said that the first boy who takes advantage of me will never have to worry about a future sex life, because he won't have one."

"Ouch! I promise to be good," I laughed. "So what's the other part?"

"You're a wrestler!"

"So!"

173

"According to Dad, all wrestlers are prima donnas, obsessively compulsive about their bodies and their diets, and all that. He thinks you are all cocky show-offs. He told me that you probably spend most of your time parading around in muscle shirts, preening in front of a mirror, and flexing your muscles. I told him that most of the time you wear nothing but loose fitting sweat shirts, but he wouldn't listen. He still remembers some nasty little ninety-eight pounder who used to strut like a banty rooster when he was a kid."

"Oh boy," I moaned. "This sounds like it's going to be fun. Tell me. Did your dad play basketball in high school by any chance?"

"Yes. Why?"

"He sounds just like some of the round ballers at our school. Which is fine, except for the fact that none of it is true?"

"Oh, I don't know about all of it being untrue. After all, you do kind of strut," she said with a grin on her face.

"Hey! Give me a break! First off, I don't strut. It's just that I'm in great shape and have good posture. My arms are kind of muscular for my body size so they hang differently. I'm not strutting! I'm just walking kind of funny because that's the way I'm built. Secondly, I'm not cocky. I do have a lot of self confidence on the wrestling mat, but I'm not in love with myself. There's a difference. If you don't go out on the mat knowing you can win, you won't. You'll get beat up on in a heartbeat. Thirdly, he might be right about some of us being a little obsessive compulsive about our diets and weight. We have to be. I wrestle at 138. If I weigh in at 138 ½, I don't wrestle. I forfeit my match which counts as a loss on my record for both me and the team. I have to watch my weight and my diet. Fortunately my natural weight is 138 so all I really have to do is maintain the status quo."

"Oh, good! I can hardly wait. You're gonna meet my dad. He's already decided that he probably doesn't like you, and now you've got a chip on your shoulder. This should be great fun!" Jamie said.

"Don't worry. Everything will be fine," I told her with a smile not believing a word of it. "If you're okay with my coming over for dinner and meeting your parents, I'll be there on my best behavior."

Oh well, at least I talked a good game. Needless to say I felt nervous as a cat about meeting her dad. I hoped her mom would at least cook something I liked. With my luck she'd serve liver. I wouldn't be able to eat it and then both her parents would hate me. I could hardly wait—not!

Chapter 16

That night in bed I lay staring at the ceiling wondering what the hell I was going to do. I just had too much on my mind. I needed Scott. I knew he couldn't come if my latest problems were petty, but at least I could talk at him telepathically and pretend like he was there. Maybe it would make me feel better anyway.

"Scottie, my boy. I'm in over my head again. I'm gonna unload on you a bit even if you aren't here and can't help. At least maybe I can work through some stuff just by talking about it. First off there's Dad. He's still in that damned coma and won't come out of it. The doctors are saying there is absolutely nothing wrong now. The CT scan shows no pressure remaining on the brain; he just has to decide that it's time to wake up. When he does, he'll be fine.

"In the meantime, Mom and I are both going nuts worrying about him. She's maybe getting four or five hours of sleep out of every twenty-four and is getting ornery as a bear. That just can't be good for her being as far along with the baby as she is and everything. I've gotten to the point where I don't care if I win this weekend or not. Between school, wrestling, Dad, Bruno, and meeting Jamie's dad tomorrow night I'm getting seriously brain dead."

"You've always been a little brain dead, if you want the honest truth," Scott said.

My eyes snapped open at the sound of his voice. Scott and Mooshy squatted at the foot of my bed grinning at me.

"You startled me!" I stammered. "When did you two get here?"

"When you started flapping your gums. I planned on coming tonight anyway. I knew things had started to pile up on you again. If you had opened your eyes, you probably would have seen our shining halos and known that we were here. We are your guardian angels, you know."

"Yeah, right! Whatever! Since when did they give out angel halos to dudes who moon school buses full of cheerleaders and dogs who dig up the neighbor's freshly planted rose bushes?"

"That's a lie and you know it. You just made that story up on the spur of the moment when your mom had you out driving. That was a terrible thing to tell her."

177

"That's okay. That's my story and I'm sticking to it," I laughed feeling some of my tension slip away.

"Besides, you can't blame Mooshy for digging up your mom's new rose bush. He just thought he knew a better place for it to be planted."

"Three times?"

"Oh well, he just wasn't sure where it would look the best. Now, let's get down to your paranoia du jour. First off, your dad's going to be fine. I'll probably have to go over to the hospital and yell at him and drag his butt out of that bed."

"He can't see you or hear you. He wouldn't know it if you did go yell at him," I said wondering what he had on his mind. He usually didn't make off handed comments like that unless he had a plan.

"I think I can get into his dreams," Scott said. "I'll have to check out the details with my mentor, but I think that's a possibility. He'll have to tell me how to do it. He told me one time that if I really needed to get a message across to someone, I could make them dream the message I wanted to give them."

"You remember Jamie Austin? I'm dating her now. I dumped Lexie. Like you said, she's bad news all around. You know what?

She ended up stealing that pair of jeans she wanted me to buy for her."

"Finally! So what made you actually jump off the Lexie pity party band wagon and tell her to take a hike?"

"When she got all huffy about my being at the hospital with Dad instead of meeting her at the food court last week on Wednesday night. She figured that since he's in a coma he wouldn't know if I were there or not and that I should just sneak out for an hour and meet her. After I broke up with her, she told me that's why she wanted me to come so she could break up with me. Go figure! Women!"

"I told you she was a real piece of work!" Scott said shaking his head.

"So guess who her latest boy friend is? Moose!"

"You're kidding! They are a perfect match for each other. One is about as ditzy as the other. So tell me what's going on with Jamie? She's always been a nice kid—kind of shy and unassuming, but very bright. Latch on to her, dude! She's a keeper."

"That's the plan, but there's a problem there too. I'm supposed to go over to her house tomorrow night for dinner. Guess what! Her dad doesn't like wrestlers. He's an old basketball player. Need I say any more?"

179

"Naw! Let me guess. You're arrogant, a bully, bulimic, muscle bound, not very bright, and can't slam dunk a basketball because of your anemic five foot eight inch height disability—which, of course, is all true."

"That just about sums it up," I said.

"Don't sweat it. I already knew about Jamie and your dinner invitation so I checked him out. He's full of bluster and BS, but he's really a pretty decent guy. Actually, he's just pulling Jamie's leg. His best friend in high school was a kid on the wrestling team—that ninety-eight pounder that he rags about strutting like a banty rooster. They were known as Mutt and Jeff around school. Dinner will be fine. He actually is pretty curious about Jamie's first real boy friend."

"Are you screwing around with me, or did you really check him out?"

"I did. Just go and act normal—as hard as that may be for you—and everything will be fine. Lose the chip on your shoulder in the meantime."

"I will. I promise, but there's something else I wanted to talk to you about. Scott, you know Mom's six months along now and I feel so selfish. I just don't know how I feel about having a baby at home. Maybe I'm just jealous or something. I've always been the only child. Well, not really. You and I shared both sets of parents so it was more like we were twins or something. Anyway, I just don't know. I've already told Mom that I'm not changing any crappy diapers."

"You're gonna love having a baby brother or sister to help nurture and watch grow. You're gonna be the big brother that we never had. I don't know what its name is yet, because the baby's sex is a secret until it's born. I do know you're going to love it to pieces and be its protector. You know, little kids are always getting into trouble and need someone to sympathize with them when the Rents come down hard. As far as the crappy diapers go, that's where Marty comes in."

Then I told him, "But Mom's getting so big it's even hard for her to stand up after she's been sitting for a while. She looks like she's giving birth to a litter, not just one little baby. She spends hours at the hospital, and I think it's time I thought more about her than my problems. I even thought about asking Marty to help me clean the house from top to bottom, but he's busy with his babysitting job."

"Okay, Bro, we'll get started on it tomorrow morning before school. Good thing you've got a half day off for teacher training or whatever it is they're doing," Scott said. "Between the two of us we'll have this place spotless in no time. I just hope your mom doesn't faint when she walks in. Let's go to bed now and start right after she leaves in the morning. I'm just letting you know now that I'm gonna work your tail off." We both laughed and it felt good. Scott was Scott and could always make me laugh and forget my troubles.

...

I guess I drove around the block maybe three times before pulling into Jamie's driveway at exactly five o'clock. I did not look forward to this at all. She met me at the door with a smile on her face. She always wears a big smile around me. She's so pretty, and I was so glad to see her, that I almost forgot about my nervousness. Almost, not quite!

After the introductions were over, Jamie's mom suddenly needed her to help in the kitchen. That left me alone in the living room with Mr. Austin. Oh, boy!

"So, Jeremy, first off I want to tell you how sorry I am about your father. However, Jamie tells me that he's right on the edge of coming out of his coma so hopefully that will happen real soon."

"Thanks," I replied. "It's really been beating both of us up. My mom's so tired she can hardly function. She's gone back to work every day and then spends half the night at the hospital. I just don't know how she does it. I try to get up there every night from seven to nine just to give her a little breather. It doesn't help much, but I do the best I can."

"That's great," he said. "Jamie tells me that your family is very close. I really like to see that. It seems like so many families tend to have everyone go their own way today. Anyway, to change the subject just a little bit, I understand that you're a wrestler and going to regionals this weekend. You must be pretty good. What's your record?"

"Right now I'm at 45 and 2 for the season so that puts me in good shape for the tournament. The two kids that beat me have both gone up a weight so Marty will have to contend with them, and he's already beaten both in other tournaments this year so hopefully we'll both go a long ways."

"That's super! I hope both of you go all the way. Now let me ask you something that has been bugging me for twenty years. You know that thing where you wrestlers lie on your back and then roll back on your head lifting all your weight off the floor and onto your neck until you touch the mat with your nose? What's the trick? During my senior in high school, my best friend wrestled 98 pounds, and he was a cocky little turd. He always told me that it demonstrated brute, animal strength that the typical basketball player couldn't possibly be expected to understand. He would tell me point blank to my face that we were all nothing but a bunch of pussies. And that guy was my best friend! Can you imagine what the other wrestlers thought of us?"

I laughed. He sounded like it still bothered him after twenty years. "Really, there's no big trick to it. Your buddy exaggerated a bit maybe, but it does relate to the conditioning and strength you develop over the years. We practice with people lying on our chests pretending that they are trying to pin us. The object, of course, is to be able to lift your shoulders off the mat when you're on your back using your neck muscles, and then do a spin move so that you land on your belly and don't get pinned. So what I do in practice is rock back until I kiss the mat and then spin with Marty lying over the top of me. Then we switch off and he does the same thing."

"You're B.S.'ing me. You can't go back and kiss the mat with someone your own weight lying on you."

"Yes I can," I said.

"You've got to show me. I don't believe it."

"I can't really do it the way I am now. I've got a dress shirt on so I'd have to take it off and I don't have a tee shirt on under it."

"Big deal! Everyone around here has seen bare-chested boys. I want to see you kiss the mat."

So I did. I took off my shirt, got down on the floor and rolled around a little bit warming up my neck muscles. Once I was loose, I flipped over on my back, did a bridge, and kissed the mat. He stood there with his mouth open and said he couldn't believe it. Then he asked if I could actually do it if Jamie was lying across my chest. I told him sure, but she might be more comfortable with it if she just sat on me.

"Jamie! Come in here a minute please," he called out.

"What are you guys doing?" she laughed as she saw me lying on the floor with no shirt on grinning at her.

"Sit down on my lower chest right about at the sternum," I told her. "I have to prove a point to your dad."

When she did, I couldn't help but to show off just a little. I rocked back and forth three times kissing the mat. Then I told her, "Get ready, Jamie, you're going for a bumpy ride."

With that, I did a quick spin flopping down to my belly sending her bouncing across the carpet screaming.

"What is going on here?" Mrs. Austin exclaimed rather loudly. "I walk into my living room to see my daughter sitting on a muscular, half naked boy just before he sends her flying across the living room. What am I missing here?"

"A demonstration of brute, animal strength that no basketball player could ever expect to understand," Mr. Austin said laughing. Then he reached down and grabbed my hand and pulled me to my feet. "Jamie, get him a washcloth and towel and show him where the bathroom is. He's all hot and sweaty and I'm sure he'd like to rinse off and cool down a little before we eat."

Dinner was great. We had beef stroganoff, green beans, and mandarin oranges—all my favorites. We laughed and talked all the way through. Mr. Austin even picked on me about the sloppy looking loose fitting shirt that I had on. "It has to be that way," I explained. "I have a men's small-to-medium sized body and a size 16" neck. Therefore I have to buy large shirts and sweats to get them over my head so then they look baggy."

When I left at a quarter to seven to get to the hospital, Mr. Austin not only shook my hand, but actually gave me a little hug and told me again that he wished the best for my dad and our family. I had a big smile on my face. Life was good. Now, if Dad would just wake up.

Chapter 17

On Friday evening, the night before the regional tournament started, I had a chance to be alone with Dad for about an hour. I really unloaded on him.

"Dad, I'm at the point where I really don't care if I win tomorrow or not. It really doesn't matter that much to me anymore. I just want the season to be over. I don't care if I am the number one seed. That doesn't mean squat. The only thing I want is to have you back.

"I couldn't handle losing you. I lost Scott last year and I'm not gonna lose you! Damn it! Don't just lay there. Do something! Say something!"

Of course he didn't, but I railed at him until Mom relieved me at nine. She could tell I was upset when she came in, but she didn't say anything about it.

"Go home and get some sleep, Honey. Tomorrow's going to be a huge day," She said as she gave me a hug.

So I did. Pretty much resigned to my fate, I crawled into bed, rolled over, and went right to sleep. Scott and Mooshy didn't even show up to try to make me feel better. They didn't even care about me and my problems anymore. To hell with them!

Saturday morning came with a flurry, and, as usual, everything was crazy. I hadn't slept restfully at all so that sure didn't help my frame of mind. I'd gone right to sleep, but then I kept waking up every half hour or so all night. Not a great way to spend the night before the biggest wrestling tournament of my life.

Weigh-ins started at nine a.m. with wrestling scheduled to begin at eleven. I had no problems making weight so I could eat breakfast as soon as I certified. Marty and I rode with Jim Dad and Mom Sara so everyone arrived early. They both helped out by setting up the wrestler's table in the cafeteria and straightening up all of our gear and belongings. Mom didn't expect to come until eleven or a little after. Marty and I spent the time after we arrived eating and hanging out together. Ashley and Jamie planned to drive down later and would get there just before wrestling started.

Marty spent most of the time trying to get me pumped up. "You know," he said, "Coach told me that if we both get out of the regional tournament as first seeds, it'll be the first time in our school's history that two kids have gone to the states favored to win."

"Just because we're first seeds doesn't mean we'll be favored," I told him. "There are four regionals all placing kids in the tournament."

"I know, but we've both been keeping track of records and you know as well as I do that ours are about the best. We could both win states this year."

"Yeah! Yeah! And crows fly north for the winter. Where are Ashley and Jamie? I thought they'd be here by now."

"Ashley's babysitting Bobby so all three of them should get here right about eleven."

"He's so funny," I said. "He'll be running all over the place socializing with all the wrestlers whether he knows them or not."

"I know. He's a great kid. Just think. In about ten years we'll be going to his meets," Marty said with a far off smile on his face.

Competition finally started a few minutes after eleven. Still not able to get psyched up for my first match, I barely won the thing 4-2. I should have mopped up the floor with that kid.

My second match found me flat on my back with both shoulder blades in contact with the mat as the referee slapped it. For the first time all season, some dude pinned me, and I really didn't care. Marty took it harder than I did. Mom still hadn't showed up. I couldn't help but wonder why. She said she'd be here. Had something happened? Is there a problem with Dad?

If I lost again, I'd be done and wouldn't go to states. Somehow, I managed to win my third match. However after the first period of the fourth match, I was down by a score of 6-2. Things didn't look too good. I had the down position as we positioned ourselves for the second period. In that split second from when I froze in place and the referee dropped his hand with the command, "Wrestle!" Scott appeared.

He squatted on his hands and knees mirroring my position about three feet in front of my nose with the biggest scowl I've ever seen on him. "Get your head out of your ass!" he screamed at me. "If you blow this tournament without even trying, you'll never forgive yourself. Look over my left shoulder at the hallway, you idiot! LOOK!" he screamed at me again as loud as he could.

"Where?" I mouthed to myself.

I looked. I saw Mom in the hallway along with Jim Dad who was pushing a wheelchair right towards the mat. Dad sat in the wheelchair pumping his fist into the air at me.

190

"Wrestle!" the referee said as he dropped his hand.

I flew into the wildest fury I ever experienced. I escaped from his grasp and stood up on my feet. In the same motion I dove at his legs, spun, and dumped him on his back. I scrambled up on top of him, threw in a half nelson, and pinned the kid in less than twenty seconds into the second period. By the time they raised my hand in victory, Jim Dad had parked and braked Dad's wheelchair at the edge of the mat. I flew off the mat and dove into his arms. Good thing Jim Dad stood behind the chair with a death grip on it, or we probably would have both landed in a heap on the floor.

That evening when we were all settled in at the restaurant, Dad told me how it happened. "The thing I remember the clearest is you sitting with me for a while last night telling me that you didn't really care if you won or lost. It wasn't important to you anymore. That really bothered me. I struggled to wake up and get to your meet today, but I just couldn't do it. I faded off again.

"Then a really strange thing happened. This morning I had a dream. In the dream I saw Scott and Mooshy sitting at the foot of my bed glaring at me looking very ornery. Then Scottie started scolding me. He told me that you had given up, and that I had to wake up and get to the tournament. That would be the only way you'd have a chance. After six years on the mat you deserved to get to the highest place that you were capable of and that you weren't going to do it without me. Then they both stood up and

191

gave me another stern look as Scott told me to wake the hell up and go support my kid. Then they disappeared. For some reason or the other, their expressions and attitudes struck me funny. I woke up laughing right as your mom walked into my room."

Scott came through again. He still cared. We all sat there without speaking and just listened as Dad continued with the story. The doctors insisted on running a whole bunch of tests on him, and he threatened to just walk out. Finally this afternoon they gave him the okay and Mom and Dad headed for the tournament. Mom called Jim Dad on the way, and he met them at the door and took over wheelchair duties.

He looked over at me and said, "Jeremy, I can't thank you enough for helping your mom by cleaning the house. It really helped. She said you even cleaned the refrigerator out and all the cupboards. I am very proud of you."

"As am I," Mom said, "and I want to thank you very much. I hate to tell you, but I called Sara to thank her and she didn't know what I was talking about. Then she said that she saw you taking a bunch of things out to the trash but didn't think anything of it. I just don't know how you did that all by yourself in such a short time." Then she gave me that funny smile.

I made up some story about how bored and restless I'd been and needed to burn off some excess energy. Then I told her that as soon as wrestling was over in just one more week I could help her a lot more. "I'm sure that after the baby comes you'll need all the help you can get, but I still say, when it comes to poopy diapers, NOT!"

What really freaked me out was when I tried to introduce Dad to Jamie, he told me that they had already met. "I know Jamie. She came up to the hospital several times and talked to me every time. You don't have to introduce us. We're already friends."

Jamie set me back a little too later when we were alone. "I had the binoculars on you when your dad came in. The expression on your face was one of complete resignation and defeat, and I really felt bummed for you. I just knew you didn't have a chance. Just before the referee dropped his hand, your head jerked up and you suddenly had this really intense look on your face, and you mouthed something that looked like 'Where?' What happened right then? It's obvious that you saw your dad because when the ref blew the whistle, you wrestled like a mad man—like you should have been doing all day. But what else happened? Something did."

"Gee, I don't know," I lied. "Maybe I just caught the sight of Dad out of the corner of my eye and couldn't believe what I saw. Obviously, it fired me up." That was too close for comfort. I sure couldn't tell her what really happened, "Oh, Scott squatted there giving me hell for not fighting like I should and to check out my dad over in the doorway." Yeah, right!

That night in bed I just shut my eyes and said, "Thanks Scott. I'm sorry for what I said about you last night. I owe you one."

"And I will collect!" he answered back as I looked up and saw him and Mooshy sitting in their normal spot at the foot of the bed just before they faded out and vanished. I smiled and went immediately to sleep. The state finals were coming next week and I'd be there on the mat. Things were looking up.

Chapter 18

Monday arrived, finding Marty and I both charged up. I don't think Coach Andrews told us to pipe down in English class more than a half dozen times or so. He didn't come down too hard on us though. He totally understood. I hadn't felt this invigorated in some time. I could hardly wait for the weekend. It would be my one and only trip to the state tournament, and I was ready.

Our preparations all week were a rip. Marty and I attacked each other every night during practice like we were mortal enemies. Then we would fall back on our backs on the mat and laugh like a couple of six year olds. I don't know when I ever experienced a week like that. We busted our butts as hard as humanly possible. Also since there were only a handful of us going to the state tournament, the coaches gave us all kinds of individual attention and that helped us all the more.

Fortunately Ashley handled the babysitting duties so Marty could concentrate on getting himself ready. Of course, they did manage to get their time every night for just the two of them. After practice, dinner, and homework, Marty left the house and met up with her for at least an hour. On a couple of the nights Jamie and I tagged along. We all went to the food court at the mall. Was that every a joy! Right! The two of them sat at the table staring into each other's eyes, sneaking kisses, and whispering in each other's ears while Jamie and I tried to be cool, talk about the state tournament, and ignore them. Eventually we'd just leave them and walk the mall. We were a little shyer than those two and didn't like to make out in public. However, out in my car all by ourselves, it was a different story.

Friday morning provided the highlight of the school week. All of us going to states planned to leave in a car pool at nine in the morning. So at eight the school gave us a huge send off pep rally in the gym to launch us on our way. That totally geeked me out. When our cars pulled out of the parking lot, we were pumped. Jim Dad drove the car that Marty and I rode in. Dad wasn't a hundred per cent yet so he just chilled out in the passenger seat.

The moms wanted to drive down later in the day for the first round scheduled for two o'clock. Ashley would be riding with them. Jamie's parents decided to take a half day off of work and come to the state meet to cheer Marty and me on so she rode with them. Fortunately neither Marty nor I had any concerns with our weights so we could have breakfast and munchies on the trip. The state had scheduled weigh-ins for noon.

196

"Can you believe it" We're actually headed to the state tournament?" I said to Marty after we were on the road.

"No, I really can't. Who would've thought—after everything that has happened this year, we both made it!"

"I know. When you realize that most kids never get to this point, it's really pretty cool."

We talked most of the way keeping ourselves pumped. We arrived with a half hour to spare before we had to step up on the scale. It would be the only time for the two day tournament if we made weight.

I've mentioned before that I always found weigh-ins strange. Every meet you'd see guys running in double sweats trying to lose that last extra pound so they could qualify. Why they put themselves through that mystified me. What a bummer that would be to get all the way to the states and then not be able to wrestle because you were a pound or so too heavy.

Friday's wrestling went great for both Marty and me. We both won all of our matches meaning that we would at least get a medal no matter what. That night at dinner every one in our group was in a great mood. Marty and Ashley took over Emily so that Mom Sara could have a break. I swear they were "playing house." Oh well! I looked after Jamie so that left the old folks to fend for themselves. We didn't have to weigh in again on

197

Saturday so we both ate steak and fries along with dessert. The other guys from our school lost their matches early and left to go home. Their season was over so it was just the two of us. When Marty and I went to bed, we were both so wired that we couldn't sleep. We talked and laughed until who knows when.

First, second, and third rounds Saturday morning went like clockwork. Marty and I both won handily. That meant we had the rest of the day to screw around until finals that evening. We would both compete for the state championship. I think Marty and Ashley spent most of the afternoon in the parking lot, probably in the back seat of Jim Dad's car. I really didn't want to know what they were doing or where they were. Personally I was so revved up I couldn't relax, so Jamie and I spent most of the late afternoon just wandering around talking. No way could I have been squirreled away someplace making out all day. I just had too much nervous energy.

Late in the afternoon I sat in the balcony with Jamie, daydreaming, and watching the action below when suddenly Scott and Mooshy parked themselves beside me and watched the matches with us. Neither one of us said much. Scott and I shot a handful of telepathic messages back and forth, but that was about it.

Marty and Ashley eventually crawled out of hiding and joined us, They'd been out swapping spit someplace, but the time to start warming up for the finals had arrived. It was now or never.

Chapter 19

When the finals finally started, spectators packed the place. The girls headed back to their spots to watch with the Rents and left us on our own. Marty and I completely focused on our championship matches due to start in less than an hour. Scott and Mooshy hung out with us until match time while Marty and I psyched ourselves up. By the time we finished warming up, we were ready.

I wrestle one weight class lighter than Marty so my match went first. He stood off in the alleyway doing jumping jacks and keeping warm as he watched. Scott and Mooshy sat on the edge of the mat cheering me on while I did my prelims. Even Mooshy sat up and stayed awake. The first period I managed a takedown and ended up ahead two-zip when the buzzer sounded. Period two ended 4-2 with me in the lead. Let's do it, I thought to myself.

I wanted to end my wrestling career and championship match with a flurry. I crouched down in the bottom position starting the last period. I escaped and managed another takedown before the final horn. I won my state championship 7-2. After they raised my arm in victory, I ran across the mat and jumped into my dad's arms with a war whoop. I even let Scott give me a hug that nobody else but Bobby saw.

Marty wrestled next. Coach let me sit with him on the edge of the mat with my gold medal hanging around my neck. As he stood in the middle of the mat getting set up and ready to start, he looked at me. I pointed to my medal and yelled at him, "Go get it, Marty!"

He smiled and positioned himself for the start. As soon as the referee blew his whistle, Marty shot at his opponent's legs and earned himself takedown points right at the start. He maintained total control for the rest of the match. Half way through the third period and leading 9-0, Marty turned the kid on his back and flattened his shoulders to the mat. The whistle blew and the ref slapped the mat. Marty jumped straight up in the air with a fist pump to celebrate his victory.

When the dust cleared, it finally sunk in. Marty and I had both won our individual state championships. After they presented Marty's medal, we dressed out in our street clothes. It was time to head out. We, as well as all our families and friends who had come with us, wanted to celebrate.

Jamie's dad came over and shook my hand and gave me a hug. "Jeremy, I owe you an apology. Like I told you before, I thought that all you wrestlers were a bunch of arrogant prima donnas who were obsessed with your bodies as you strutted around like a bunch of little banty roosters. I didn't realize what all went into this sport—the skill, the strategy, the strength, the technique. I had no clue. All I can say is, I really am impressed.

"You know, I don't know what's going to happen down the road as far as you and Jamie are concerned, and today it probably doesn't really matter. However, I do want you to know that I am very proud of you. My relationship with you the past few weeks and this tournament today has been quite an eye opener for me. I had more fun watching than I could ever have imagined."

"Gee, Mr. Austin. Does that mean I don't have to grovel when I ask permission to marry Jamie someday 'down the road' as you say?"

He looked me right straight in the eye, gave me a devilish smile, and said, "Hell yes you're going to grovel! Don't think for one minute you're going to get off easy."

We all went to the guillotine when we finally made it back to town. Marty and I both ate like food was going out of style. Everyone in the place congratulated us and shook our hands acting like we were local heroes or something. Coach joined our group for a couple of minutes and gave both Marty and me a big

201

hug and told us how happy it had made him to have the opportunity to coach us.

After we thanked everyone for their support and for coming, we climbed back into our cars and went home. It had been a long six years of wrestling, a long season, and a very long day. I was tired. Now it was time to relax, have fun, get myself graduated, and have my first date with Mr. Austin. Oh, boy!

Chapter 20

With wrestling season over, March Madness and the NCAA college basketball tournament started. I had never paid a whole lot of attention other than keeping track of State and who they won and lost to in the tournament. I always filled out a bracket sheet having no idea who I had just picked or why most of the time, and the results looked like it.

Thursday night came, and I spent my time studying and thinking about Jamie. My cell phone rang. Caller ID said '*Jamie*', "Hi!" I said not even trying to hide the excitement of hearing from her. "What's going on?"

"Jeremy, don't you dare sound like you're salivating when you think its Jamie on the other end of the line! This is John Austin. What are you doing tomorrow night?"

Holy Crap! It was Jamie's dad. "Nothing important, Sir. Jamie and I talked about going to a movie or something either Friday or Saturday night, but we haven't firmed up our plans. She wants to spend most of the weekend getting ready for her Advanced Placement calc test next week, and she didn't know what your family had planned. Why?"

"Well, she can do her studying Friday night, and you two can have Saturday. State plays their first game at five thirty Friday night so why don't you come over and watch the game with me in the Man Cave? Get here about five o'clock and we'll load up on junk food and watch the game in the den."

"Sure! Sounds like fun," I said. "Can I talk to Jamie for a minute?"

"Here!" he said as he handed the phone over to Jamie. "He wants your permission."

"Hi, Jeremy! Welcome to Dad's world," she laughed.

"Hi, Jamie! Is this going to be okay with you? Can we do the movie on Saturday night? We really hadn't set an exact night for it."

"That's fine. Besides it will give you and Dad a chance to really get to know each other and bond a little. You know, he really is just a big harmless teddy bear."

204

The next day in chemistry we talked at length. Obviously I felt a little nervous as I didn't know exactly what would be expected of me. She just laughed and told me to relax and act normal.

"You know, he's never had a son like he always wanted. He's always been surrounded by females at home. You're the first boy to show up on the scene so he's experimenting too. Just come over and forget your diet. Wrestling season's over so you can pig out on the goodies, watch the game, and have fun. Hopefully State will win."

I showed up at five o'clock and Mr. Austin met me at the door. "Hi, Jeremy! Come on in. Toss your jacket in the closet over there, and let's head out to the kitchen. I'm starved!"

Mrs. Austin had filled the kitchen with food. There were the makings for Sloppy Joes, chips, dips, celery and carrot sticks, deserts, soft drinks, you name it—my kind of spread. I didn't want to look too much like a hog so I let him kind of take the lead. No problem. No way could I keep up with him so I just filled my plate and headed for the den.

"Where's Jamie?" I asked once we had settled in front of the TV. I hadn't seen her since I'd arrived.

"Oh, she's in the office on her computer trying to prepare for her AP calc test. You know, I'd never tell her, but there are disadvantages to being so darned bright. She works way too hard. She doesn't think so, but her mom and I do."

"I know," I said. "However, she does seem to get into the challenge."

"Yeah, she does. In the meantime, don't worry! She'll probably check up on you a couple of times before the game's over."

"I hope so," I said probably too quickly before feeling a quick flush on my face. Mr. Austin noticed my embarrassment and laughed. That made me even redder.

A while later Jamie slipped up behind me and started massaging the back on my neck and shoulders. "So, what's the score?" she asked.

"Tied up with less than a minute to go in the first half," I answered kind of moving my neck and shoulders in appreciation. I hoped she didn't stop.

"Hey! Didn't you see the sign? No girls allowed," Mr. Austin joked at Jamie. "This is the Man Cave. And, by the way, aren't you getting a little overly touchy-feely friendly back there?"

"Dad, you just worry about the game and don't pay any attention to what I'm doing back here behind the sofa," she teased. Then she reached down and kissed me on the cheek right there in front of him.

By then half time started and he stood up, rolled his eyes at us, and headed for the kitchen. "Time for a re-fill," he said.

"So, how's it going?" she asked as soon when he walked out the door.

"Fine. We don't exactly agree on some of the intricacies of the game, but that's what makes it fun."

"What do you mean?" she asked.

"Well, one of their guards was racing down the court in a fast break when our guy intentionally fouled him as he went up for the basket. Your dad thought the guy'd made a great play because it disrupted the other guy's shot and made him miss the basket. However, he made both of his free throws so it didn't really make any difference. I told your dad that if he had given him a hard enough karate chop across the bicep, it would've not only disrupted his shot, but it would have made it harder to shoot his free throws."

"Jeremy, dear, they don't play Commando Basketball like you and your wrestling buddies do after practice."

"Yeah, I know. It's a shame isn't it? It'd be a lot more fun."

207

"Come on! Let's go get something to eat. I'm hungry!" she said as she dragged me off the couch.

When we walked into the kitchen, Mr. and Mrs. Austin were both fixing their plates.

"Well, are you enjoying the game?" Mrs. Austin asked.

"Very definitely," I said. "Even if they do act like a bunch of wussies when they foul each other."

"Yeah, right!" Mr. Austin snorted. "I've told you two about the wrestler mentality we're dealing with here. This clown thinks they should just body slam each other when they want to disrupt a shot."

Not a bad idea, I thought laughing at the vision in my head. Anyway, it was time to head back for the second half of the game so we picked up our full plates and returned to the den. As the game started to wind down, State pulled out to a ten point lead and things looked pretty good. The other team went into the foul, stop the clock, free throw mode hoping they might have a chance to catch up. One of the fouls came on a layup and our shooter went flying and landed on his butt sliding out of bounds.

"Flop!" I shouted out just hoping to stick it to Mr. Austin a little. It worked.

"Flop! What are you talking about? That guy should be charged a technical for an intentionally hard foul."

"Wait for the replay!" I yelled back. "I'll bet he never touched him except for that little tap on the wrist. The big pussy went sprawling intentionally. Get up, you wuss, and play ball!" I yelled at the screen.

"What are you two screaming at?" laughed Jamie's as she entered the room to make sure no blood was flying.

"This idiot friend of yours thinks that guy lying on the floor with the trainer talking to him flopped. I can't believe he'd think the guy would fake it!" Mr. Austin railed.

"I'll bet he gets up like nothing happened and shoots his free throws—after he catches his breath of course," I jabbed. "Probably just out of shape and can't take the heat of the game."

About that time Mrs. Austin stuck her head in the room. "If you two can't play nicely together, you're both going to get a time out!" she said while Jamie and I laughed. Mr. Austin continued to plead his case until the guy jumped up, dusted himself off, and shot his free throws like nothing had happened.

State ended up winning by twelve and would move on to the next round Sunday afternoon. "Wanna do this again next game?" Mr. Austin asked as I put on my coat.

"Sure! I'd love to," I replied.

"Why don't you ask Marty if he'd like to come. Maybe he knows more about basketball than you do and can educate you on the finer points since you don't believe what I tell you.

"I'll check with him tonight. Want me to let you know?"

"No, just bring him along. And, Jeremy, all kidding aside, I had fun tonight."

Jamie walked me to the car, and we talked about our date for the next night. We decided to get a quick bite to eat someplace cheap and then go to the movies. She always paid her own way which made me kind of uncomfortable. I told her that wasn't the way it was supposed to be, but she wouldn't listen. She knew I lived on an allowance because there were no jobs for teenagers in this economy. Actually it meant we could do more things together if she did. I just didn't like the idea of it even if the money did come from her dad.

Saturday night we had a riot. We ended up double dating with Marty and Ashley. Marty actually got into basketball more than I did and acted real excited about our "date" with Jamie's dad on Sunday afternoon.

We rode together and showed up a half hour before the game started. A small barrel of Nachos waited for us when we arrived, and we dug in ravenously. If nothing else, Jamie's dad certainly knew how to feed teenagers.

After we had settled into the game for awhile, one of us said something about Commando Basketball. "Ok, I'll bite," Mr. Austin said. What's Commando Basketball?"

"That's basketball wrestler style. During the season, if we have a real good practice, we get to play a thirty minute game before we hit the showers. For some reason or the other, none of the basketball players ever want to join our game. We always invite them too," I explained.

"So what are the rules?" Mr. Austin asked. "If its wrestler style, how is it different?"

"Rules?" Marty asked, and then we both looked at each other wide eyed and shrugged our shoulders.

"Ok, here's the quickie version," I answered. "To start with, instead of five people per team there are closer to fifteen. Everyone plays who wants to and all at the same time. That way there're no timeouts and no substitutions. When we first started, Coach always lined us up by weight, had us count off. Then he'd assign the odd numbers to shirts and the even to skins or vice versa. After a while we more or less evolved into permanent teams so we'd just start our games instead of wasting time."

211

"You have thirty guys out on the floor all at the same time?" he asked. "Isn't that a little confusing?"

"Not really," Marty answered. "What most people think is a little confusing is the fact that we play with two basketballs. When the game starts, the skins start by inbounding a ball on one side of the gym, and the shirts toss one in on the other side."

"Yeah," I cut in. "Then Coach sets the clock for thirty minutes and away we go. Whoever scores the most baskets wins."

"How do you keep track of the points?" he asked.

"We set a team manager or one of the basketball players who are watching down at each end of the gym and they count the baskets. Sometimes we actually end up shooting two basketballs at the same basket at the same time. Now that tends to get confusing—especially when one ball hits the other in mid air and one accidentally drops through the hoop and we're not sure who shot the ball that scored."

"You know, for some reason or the other it doesn't really seem fair. The little guys would never get a chance to get their hands on the ball with so many people out there."

"Wrong!" I said. "Tommy Jenkins, our 98 pounder probably scores more points than anyone else."

"Yeah, but he cheats," Marty snorted.

"No he doesn't," I said defending Tommy. "Where does it say in the rules of basketball that a player can't sit on the shoulders of someone else during the game?"

"What?" Mr. Austin asked totally confused.

"Yeah, Tommy sits on the shoulders of our 198 pounder for most of the game while Eric, our 105 pounder, rides the shoulders of our heavyweight. They get all the slam dunks and shot blocks," Marty told him.

"Oh, brother!" Mr. Austin exclaimed. "Sounds like some game. So who calls fouls?"

"Fouls?" I asked.

"Yeah!" Marty laughed "Remember? Coach called one early this year when Tommy stood up to slam dunk a ball and someone reached up and pulled his sweats down. Coach claimed it was unsportsman like conduct and gave Tommy two free throws. Of course he missed both of them, but that didn't matter. He had to shoot them sitting on Curt's shoulders—just kinda awkward probably."

By the time we finished telling him all about Commando Basketball, even Mr. Austin was laughing and shaking his head. He

213

understood perfectly why the basketball players wanted no part of our game. He said that their coach probably barred them from participating afraid someone would get maimed for life playing our stupid game.

State won the game and moved on to the Sweet Sixteen next week. When Marty and I left, both Mrs. Austin and Jamie were shaking their heads and rolling their eyes. We'd had a great time and apparently made enough noise so that the ladies knew it. When we walked out the door, little did we realize the troubles that lay ahead.

Chapter 21

Life was good. Wrestling season had finished so I could eat anything I wanted to and not worry about my weight—just zits. With no practice after school, Jamie and I spent almost every afternoon together at the mall hanging out with our friends, snacking, walking the mall, and just having fun. Marty and Ashley didn't come every day because of his babysitting duties. He had his hands full.

Wednesday nights after dinner the two of us tried to do something special together for an hour or two provided we weren't loaded down with home work. I picked her up at seven and she said I had to go in and say, "Hi," to her parents before we left. Her mom always acted real nice, and her dad always acted like her dad—a character.

"And just exactly what are your intentions with my daughter in the middle of the night on a school night?" he asked giving me the evil eye.

"Dad!" Jamie scowled as she rolled her eyes and shook her head. "We'll be back by nine—give or take a couple of hours."

"We'll be back early," I said smiling.

"You still didn't tell me what your intentions are. Some things don't take all that long especially at your age," he said cocking his head down and giving me a wide open eye look.

"Mom! Can't you do anything with him?" Jamie protested.

"He's such a trusting soul," I commented as we headed for the car.

"He likes you. Can you imagine how he'd act if he didn't?"

"Oh, boy! He'd be a joy wouldn't he?" I answered as we headed out.

We had already decided earlier that we would head for the pit. Jamie and I had been there a couple of times and usually all we did was walk and talk. We'd run through a takeout someplace and pick up a couple of soft drinks and then just go and have fun for an hour or two. There was a path that wound all the way

216

around the little lake. It ran for about three miles total. A lot of couples just killed an hour or so by walking the path, holding hands, and talking. Naturally there were a number of side trails off the beaten path that you could take a little time out on if you wanted a little diversion. The best part of being there was that we were by ourselves.

We had walked for a little over an hour when we sauntered around the last bend. I looked up and saw someone leaning against the trunk of my car talking to some girl. "Oh! Oh!" I said to Jamie. "Look who's sprawled out on my car with a forty-five ouncer in his hand."

"How nice!" Jamie retorted. "Looks like we have company. Looks like Moose and some girl."

"And who do you think the girl might be?" I asked with a smirk on my face.

"Have no clue," Jamie answered.

"None other than dear Alexis herself. Why do I get the impression that this is not exactly a social call."

"Wonderful!" she said not liking the scene one bit.

As we neared the car, Moose made a point of finishing off his beer and wiping his mouth with his shirt sleeve as he belched loudly.

"Classy guy," Jamie said under her breath as we approached. "Does he chew tobacco too?"

"Well, well! If it isn't Moose and Alexis. And to what do we owe this honor?" I asked probably sounding as sarcastic as I felt.

"You get the honor of having me kick your ass, smart mouth!" Moose growled trying to sound like the bully he always tried to be.

"Moose, what exactly is your problem? I asked talking down to him like he was the village idiot. "I haven't seen you for over a year, and suddenly you show up and want to fight? Are you trying to impress Lexie or what?"

"Listen, you little bastard. You screwed me up big time with Hannah last year. I don't know what you did or how you did it because she wouldn't tell me, but she got so freaked out that she ended up telling all kinds of lies about me to our parents, the principal, and to the police. We both ended up getting sent away for a year, and now she won't even answer my emails or phone messages. I love her and she won't have anything to do with me. I don't even know where she is," he yelled out at me almost blubbering in his beer.

"What do you mean you love her? You said you love me!" Lexie screamed at him.

"Oh, just shut the hell up, you dumb bitch!" he yelled back at her before turning his attention back to me. "See what you do? You cause me nothing but trouble. Well, I've had it with you. I'm gonna cut you to shreds! See what that pretty little girl friend of yours thinks of your ugly face when I get through with it. Then I'm gonna cut up that slut after I take her out in the woods and have a little fun with her. Let's see what you think of her then!" he roared as he reached down and broke his bottle on a large rock behind him.

Then he lunged at Jamie who stood a couple of feet away and grabbed her breast. Before I could even react, she reached up and raked his face with her nails and clawed him good. Then he jumped back and with a glazed look in his eyes, whirled around facing me and started slashing that bottle at me. His attack on Jamie had pissed me off. It was one thing to threaten me, but he threatened and grabbed Jamie as well.

I instinctively threw up my arm to protect myself, and then flew into a rage. Acting on pure reflex, I reached down and grabbed his right ankle and jerked it up into a perfect wrestling move known as an ankle pick. Without even thinking about it, I spun around and blocked his left foot with my left and reefed on him as hard as I could. He went down on his back like a ton of bricks—all two hundred and thirty pounds.

219

The biggest difference between this takedown and the ones I had done hundreds of times over the years on a wrestling mat is that there are no large rocks on a wrestling mat. As his back hit the ground, I heard a huge whoosh of air and then a dull thud when his head hit that rock that he had just broken the bottle on. He didn't move. Lexie screamed at the top of her lungs while I hauled off and kicked him as hard as I could. Jamie grabbed a hold of me and pulled me back to keep me from kicking him again. That snapping sound I heard in when I buried my foot into his rib cage sounded like music. I wanted to hear it again.

"Moose!" I screamed. "Don't you ever touch or threaten Jamie again! You can threaten me all you want, but if you ever touch Jamie again, I'll break your freaking neck!" Rational thinking didn't appear to be one of my strong points right then. Moose lay on the ground out cold and couldn't hear a word I said.

"Jeremy! Jeremy! Stop it! You're bleeding and he's bleeding and unconscious. Stop it! Pull yourself together!" Jamie yelled as she held on and shook me. She was strong! I started to calm down until I saw the blood all over her top. Then I panicked.

"Jamie, you're bleeding!" I yelled. "Did that bastard cut you with that bottle?"

"No! This is your blood. Now settle down! Take off your shirt. We've got to stop that bleeding."

By then quite a crowd had gathered. A couple of people tended to Moose. Head wounds have a tendency to bleed like a stuck hog, and Moose really kind of fit the image. A couple of other kids came over and helped Jamie take care of me. I had this huge gash running from my shoulder across my chest bleeding profusely. I'm not sure how he managed to cut me the way he did because when I saw him start his slashing move, I threw up my arm and ducked. I never felt it. They made me sit down on the ground and lean against a tree as one of them held my sweat shirt against the wound as a compress trying to make the blood stop. Sirens wailed in the back ground headed our way. Damn! Jamie sat beside me and held my head while periodically kissing my cheek. That part was good, but the trouble I knew I was in, wasn't.

I have no idea who called 911, or what they said, but two ambulances arrived on the scene. I don't know why. I sure didn't think I needed one. All I wanted to do was stop the bleeding and get out of there. They could take care of Moose and leave me alone. Right! It didn't work out that way. One of the ambulance crews took care of Moose and the other hovered over me. The first thing they did was remove my sweat shirt compress and look at the damage.

"Oooh! That's kind of nasty. Gonna hurt when the shock wears off," one of them said. I didn't need to hear that.

Before I knew it, they had me lying on my back on a blanket as they applied pressure to the cut and wrapped it. It was colder

221

than hell out there to be lying on nothing but a blanket on the ground with no shirt. My teeth were even chattering! The next thing I knew they brought something out of the ambulance that looked like a combination stretcher and wheel chair and set it up beside me. As they made their final preparations, I looked up and there stood Detective Sergeant Sean O'Connor with his arms folded over his chest, glaring at me while shaking his head. Definitely not who I wanted to see right then.

"What in hell have you gone and gotten yourself into this time?" he growled not really expecting an answer.

Before they hauled me away, I gave Jamie my car keys so she could drive my car and follow the ambulance to the hospital. I also called Dad. Definitely a call I looked forward to—not!

"Dad," I said tentatively as he answered the phone. "You've got to go to the Mercy Hospital emergency room. They're getting ready to put me in the ambulance right now. I'm not hurt bad— just kind of cut up a little bit. It's not bleeding any more so I'm okay. They just won't let me drive home right now. Jamie's taking my car to the hospital." I stopped talking and waited for the explosion. It came.

"Where are you?" he yelled into the phone. "What happened? Did you get into an accident? Damn it! Answer me!"

"Dad! I'm trying to. Stop yelling at me for a second and listen! I'm at the gravel pit with Jamie. Moose showed up with a broken beer bottle and wanted to cut both Jamie and me up. I'm really okay and she didn't get hurt. The ambulance driver said you have to come and get me at the hospital and show our insurance cards. Bring me a change of clothes too. All my stuff's bloody. But I've got to go. They want to put me in the ambulance now."

"Jeremy, give me the phone and let me talk to your dad a minute," Sean said as he took the phone away from me.

"Mr. Wright, this is Sergeant Sean O'Connor. Jeremy isn't hurt too badly, but he does need to go to the hospital for stitches and maybe a transfusion. Who knows! He's lost a fair amount of blood and I see some of the signs of shock setting in. He tried to downplay his injuries when he told you about it just a bit. Like I said, he isn't critical, but he is injured and needs attention. They are getting ready to transport him now so it would be helpful if you would meet him at Mercy."

Dad said that he would head that way immediately so they picked up the thing I sat on and slid it into the ambulance. One of the attendants climbed into the back with me and took my blood pressure, all my vitals, and then stuck an IV into my arm. I had no clue why he did that. I thought I was just scraped up a little. After that, he secured the stretcher so it wouldn't move all over the place, and away we went. I could hear the driver reporting into the hospital letting them know that we were in route. Just like in

223

the movies, only, this time it was for real. I could have done without the flashing lights and sirens.. That embarrassed me even more. Ambulances ride about like a truck with no shocks cruising through Afghan foothills—rough!

The nurse was still in the process of washing me up and scrubbing out the wounds when Mom and Dad walked into my little cubical. Jamie handed Dad my car keys and started backing out. I think she was half afraid that Dad would start yelling again right there in the emergency room.

"You don't have to leave," he told her smiling. "You are kind of a mess yourself. Did you get hurt in this thing?"

"No, it's all Jeremy's blood that's on me," she said.

The nurse who was practically bathing me looked up at Jamie, "Honey, you should have someone bring you some clean clothes. You'll probably want to leave those bloody things here so we can incinerate them along with this guy's. Actually, we can just bag up your clothes and send them home with you if you prefer. That's what we normally do even if it would be safer from a health standpoint to burn all of them."

"I've already called my parents to bring me some clean clothes," she told her. "And there is no need to burn any of my stuff. It's only Jeremy's blood. I'll take them home with me and wash them."

"Doesn't matter whose blood it is. You don't know what kind of disease he might be harboring. Why do you think I'm dressed the way I am. All of this stuff touching his blood gets destroyed in a regular blast furnace. He could have AIDS; there are a number of STD's he could have; he could have TB; he could have any number of infectious diseases. Blood is nothing to mess around with. Who knows what this guy's been up to."

"Hey! We're talking about my blood here. There's nothing wrong with it," I proclaimed a bit heatedly.

"Jeremy, just be quiet and listen for a change. You might learn something." Dad said annoyed at my interruption. "They don't know you from Adam around here. You're just the next clown who got himself messed up and needs to be patched up. You could have anything or everything. They have to take all the safety precautions they can to protect themselves and others like Jamie who just happen to be covered with someone else's body fluids."

Dad was right, as usual, so I shut up. Just then, another pair of doctors, nurses, technicians, or whoever they were walked in. I'm not quite sure who they were. However, I was much happier when they left. "This is going to sting just a little," one of them said as they brought out this huge needle. "You have any pirates in your family tree? When we get through putting in your stitches, you'll fit right in."

225

Very funny! Just what I needed—a bunch of comedians sewing me up I thought to myself. They numbed me up all over the cut area from my shoulder all the way across my chest. Needles in the chest don't just sting, they hurt! However, by the time they started stitching me up, nothing smarted anymore thank goodness. I was completely numb. I had no idea how many stitches they put in, and I really didn't care. The important thing, at least to me, was they said that I probably wouldn't have much of a scar.

That was good news. The bad news was the tetanus shot. That hurt too. I think every single thing they did to me hurt. Also the fact that they wanted to keep the IV in so they could keep pumping fluids into me and make me stay the night for observation didn't do much for my mind set either. They wanted to keep tabs on me for shock and who knows what else. However, I started getting so tired it really didn't matter. What did matter was the bad news to follow.

Chapter 22

About that time Sean walked in. "Guess what?" he said. "Good thing you're staying here tonight 'cause you can't go anywhere until we get some legal things cleared up. Moose's dad wants to press charges against you for assault with the intent of doing great bodily harm less than murder."

"What? He's the one who attacked me!" I yelled. "He cut me with a broken beer bottle and then grabbed and threatened Jamie. If anyone presses charges it's gonna be me."

"Calm down and listen for a minute. Dropping him on his head on the rock and knocking him out was self defense. Raring back and kicking him in the ribs and threatening to break his freaking neck at the top of your lungs could be considered as assault with the intent of doing great bodily harm in a court of law if he hires a good lawyer who can suck up to a jury. That's what I'd like to prevent. I really don't want this going to court. You never know what's going to happen if something goes to a jury. What I do know is that you will never get accepted to State next year if you have a felony on your record."

We talked for a while making sure he had the entire story from my point of view. Dad hadn't heard about my kicking Moose in the ribs and breaking a few of them prior to Sean mentioning it. For some reason or the other, he didn't act real impressed. Anyway, before Sean headed back down the hall, he had our guarantee that we would not press charges if they didn't.

About that time Jamie's dad showed up with a change of clothes proclaiming rather loudly that she was a complete mess. She just smiled at him, took her clothes, and headed to the ladies room. While she was gone Dad caught Mr. Austin up on the details. He didn't seem overly pleased that we had been out to the pit when it all happened. I knew I hadn't heard the last of it from him or Dad.

Then we just hung around then and talked. I went into the bathroom and dressed into my nice clean sexy hospital gown. Mom tied up the back to keep the draft out, and then we waited for them to send me to my room for the night. At that point in time I didn't care. Exhausted, I just wanted to sleep. I felt weak. Somebody said it was probably caused from the loss of blood. Right then I didn't care. I could barely keep my eyes open.

After dozing on and off for about an hour, Sean came back on the scene. "Everything's taken care of," he said. "Nobody's filing any charges."

"So what happened back there?" Dad asked.

"Well, when Moose's dad stormed into the hospital ranting and raving, he was ticked. He thought that Moose had been attacked by some adult bully and beaten to a pulp. He wanted to file charges right on the spot. After things settle down, and I mentioned that a court case would involve months of trial preparation and the necessity of Alexis staying available as a material witness that the truth started to spill out.

"Lexie turned the tables on Moose and called him a loser and accused him of attacking Jeremy. She said that there was no way that she would hang around and testify for him. Her dad had just accepted a job in North Dakota and they planned to move there almost immediately. She couldn't believe some kid a hundred pounds lighter than Moose could whip his butt the way Jeremy had. Then she went on and on about how Moose had always told her that he loved her, and it had all been a lie. He had just used her for her body. He really loved someone else. She was not a happy camper. That's when she stormed out crying."

"So did Moose's dad ever get all the facts?" Dad asked.

"Well, yes. I told him the witnesses' report of the story—slipping in the fact that you maybe weigh a hundred and forty pounds soaking wet. Nobody'd told him yet about Moose attacking you with a broken beer bottle either. Seems like maybe Moose failed to mention that. That's when his dad jumped on Moose wanting to know where he'd gotten the beer. Moose hung his head and admitted he'd stolen it out of their refrigerator."

"That must have made his day," Dad said with a smile.

"Yes it certainly did. Then about that time Moose started crying and carrying on about how Jeremy had driven his girlfriend away from him a year ago. He'd been in love with Hannah forever when Jeremy somehow screwed that all up for him. Jeremy had said or done something to Hannah that totally spooked her so she would have nothing to do with him. She blamed Moose for all her troubles—including the military school prison she was stuck into just like him. Then he whined about the wasted year at the academy and how it was all Jeremy's fault. All he wanted to do was get even for the year of hell that Jeremy had put him through. He really hadn't intended to hurt either one of too badly," he said looking at me, "just maybe cut you up a little bit—just enough to scare you. He only wanted to cut Jamie up enough to make her hate Jeremy and have nothing to do with him. Needless to say, he didn't sound real rational."

"So how did his dad take it hearing the truth come out?" Dad asked.

"He just shook his head, and said ok, as far as he was concerned Moose's future was settled. It seems that he had already made arrangements for Moose to go to Texas to work on his uncle's ranch as soon as school gets out. However, since Moose had managed to fail all his classes and wouldn't be graduating anyway, and then with this situation, there'd be no reason to wait. If you agreed not to press charges, Moose would probably head to Texas this weekend about three months ahead of schedule."

Right about then an orderly wheeled a cart into my space so he could load me up and move me to my room for the night. As Jamie and her dad gathered up her stuff and prepared to leave, Mr. Austin looked at me with a very serious expression on his face. "Jeremy, when they get you up to your room, you might want to go into the bathroom where there's a mirror and freshen up your lip stick. You seemed to have smeared yours quite badly during the fight."

"Oh, Dad!" Jamie exclaimed. "Behave yourself for a change!"

Everyone laughed much to my chagrin. Apparently all of them had noticed Jamie's lipstick smeared all over my cheek and nobody bothered to say anything about it. While we were still at the pit she kept kissing me as she cradled my head as other people held the compresses on my shoulder and chest until the ambulance arrived.

Before heading out the door, she leaned down and gave me a full, extended kiss right on the mouth. "See you tomorrow, Jeremy. Sleep well and dream really, really pleasant dreams about me tonight," she said giving her dad a wide open innocent expression that just dared him to make a comment about that line.

With that she told everyone goodbye, looked over her shoulder at her dad and said, "Are you coming?"

He laughed, shook his head, and said, "That's my girl!" and away they went.

...

After Mom and Dad left, and I had settled in and had almost drifted off to sleep, I stretched out and felt something at the foot of the bed. Surprise! Surprise! There sat Scott and Mooshy.

"I can't leave you for a minute can I?" Scott whined.

"So where were you this afternoon, O'Guardian Angel of mine, taking harp lessons? I could have used a little help out there."

"You never called me. That's why. I wouldn't have been around spying on you and Jamie so I wouldn't even know you were in trouble unless you called."

"So how'd you find out?" I asked.

"My mentor told me you were in trouble again and where you were, so I went to the pits to check up on you. The ambulance was just pulling out when I arrived so I hung around to see what Sean planned to do. I pretty much know the whole story about what happened.

"Sean talked to everyone who was still on the scene after both ambulances left. Another couple had been walking the path from the opposite direction of you and Jamie. They came into the clearing right when Moose broke the bottle and attacked you. They were close enough to see and hear everything that happened, but not close enough to help stop it because it all went down so fast. They described your kicking him in the ribs and the disgusting snapping noise it made. The guy thought it was humorous—especially when you reared back to kick him again and Jamie stopped you."

"You mean Sean had other eyewitnesses to the whole thing and didn't say anything about it? Why?"

"He kept that information up his sleeve just in case he needed it. He wanted to break Moose down in front of witnesses so he'd admit to everything keeping his dad from charging you in the process. Luckily, his dad's an honest and decent guy and wanted to do the right thing. Sean looks out for you big time, but you gotta realize, that stupid attempted field goal with Moose's

233

ribcage could have backfired big time on you—especially if you'd done it a second time."

"I do now. I just never thought. He grabbed Jamie and threatened to cut her, and I freaked out simple as that."

"Well, anyway, everything worked out. There won't be any law suits, and we've gotten rid of Alexis and Moose permanently. Now, if we could just keep you from getting yourself into trouble, maybe life could move on more smoothly."

"Goodnight, Scott, you horrible ass nag," I said grinning as I rolled over on my side.

"Goodnight, Bro! Sleep well," Scott said as I drifted off to sleep.

However, that wasn't the end of the lectures. There were more to come.

Chapter 23

When I woke up the next morning Scott and Mooshy had already disappeared, and I ached all over. That paramedic sure hadn't lied when he'd said it was going to hurt. I would have hated to have anyone try to give me a hug right then. Of course, there were exceptions. If Jamie had been there, I would have managed.

Breakfast arrived at seven-thirty. Not bad, I must say. They served me eggs, toast, bacon, fried potatoes, orange juice, and skimmed milk. Ugh! I like good old fashioned whole milk with lots of unhealthy butter fat in it. I was just finishing up when a voice sounded in the doorway, "Damn, Ashley. We're late for breakfast, and the hog didn't even save us any."

She and Marty bounded into the room wearing big grins on their faces. "How on earth did you get yourself into this mess?" Ashley asked shaking her head.

"Don't you know? It's known in some circles as attempted hanky-panky," Marty laughed. "That's what happens when you go sneaking off to the gravel pit with Jamie un-chaperoned by more mature adult friends like us."

"Oh, quick! Find the bedpan. I think I'm goona puke!" as I feigned a quick barf into my hands.

"So, tell us all about it," Marty said after we quit laughing.

"First off, check out my new pirate camouflage," I told them pulling my hospital gown over showing my totally bandaged chest. Then I pulled back the dressing so they could see the stitches and redness.

After all the appropriate comments like, "Ow!" and "Yuck!" and "Gross?" They listened intently while I rehashed the previous night. I told them everything including all the gory details and how it all worked out. Marty thought breaking three of Moose's ribs with that kick was hilarious. He's the only one. Ashley reacted like everyone else. She found the fight out of character for me, and it seemed to bother her about how, in one split second of rage, I could've screwed myself up for life if Moose's dad had pressed charges and won his case.

They hung around until about twenty to nine when they had to head for school. They'd already skipped their first hour government class. "We'll make sure everyone gets the embroidered version about what a stud you are," Marty said as they prepared to leave.

"Don't, Marty. I could end up looking like the bad guy in this whole mess. Here I am still in perfect shape with wrestling only being over for a short time, and then there is Moose. He's out of shape, fatter than hell, slow as a mud turtle, and dumber than a box of rocks. He would have no chance in a fair fight, much less one where he's been drinking with an opponent totally geeked on adrenalin."

"Good speech, Jeremy. I'll try to remember it when I spread the news to all the round ballers that you just don't piss off a wrestler if you want to stay in one piece," he laughed as the two of them headed out the door.

"Well, at least you have one fan with your attempted field goal using Moose as the football," hooted Scott who suddenly appeared again at the foot of the bed looking at my chart.

"When did you get back?" I asked, "And what are the two of you doing here now? You already gave me a hard time last night for my little screw up."

"We came to cheer on the nurse when she comes in to change your bandage this morning," he said. "We want to watch as she rips that baby off and makes you scream bloody murder."

237

"Thanks, Bro. Just what I need—a cheering section. That can't be the only reason you came."

"No, we just thought we'd come and keep you company until your mom gets here to take you home at noon. Last I heard that's when they're booting your ass out of here."

So they did. We just sat around B.S.'ing each other until the nurse came in to change my bandages and check for infection, bleeding, and all that good stuff. From what I could see looking down my nose trying to watch, everything looked flaming red, crimped because of the stitches, and felt really, really sore. However, must be everything looked pretty normal to her because all she did was apply new antiseptic and re-bandage it. Fortunately, she couldn't hear the peanut gallery egging her on to "rip those babies off—and use rubbing alcohol, not that sissy stuff. Give that sucker some real pain!" Even Mooshy had to stick his cold, wet nose on my bare skin making me jump while he checked out the stitches. The nurse apologized thinking she'd hurt me.

Mom came about eleven thirty to get all the discharge instructions and to bail me out of the place. Scott and Mooshy disappeared as soon as she showed up. According to the person who released me, I had to go to my own doctor in one week to get the stitches out with all kinds of orders to get back to emergency if there were any red streaks, pussy discharges, or I started running a fever.

Mom looked and acted so tired. She seemed to be getting awfully big. She kept saying, "Three more months of this!"

The next week or so were pretty low key. My chest still hurt big time so I didn't do a whole lot except for school and hang out with Jamie. On Saturday night State played in the NCAA final four game about a hundred miles away. Somehow, through work Dad scored enough tickets for him, Jim Dad, Mr. Austin, Marty, and me. We all rode together in Jim Dad's van and had a ball. State lost the game, but the trip to the game was well worth it. When you think of all the hundreds of college teams there are in the country, and the fact that your team makes it to the final four in the country, that's pretty cool.

The following Wednesday night Marty, Ashley, Jamie, and I went to the mall to just hang out and do our mid-week relaxation gig. We were just sitting there talking and sipping on our drinks when Sean O'Connor strolled up out of uniform, grabbed a chair from the table next to ours, and sat down.

"Mind if I join you?" he asked. It was kind of a moot question because he already had.

We all said, "Hi," and, "Of course you're welcome to join us," or something close to that.

"We need to talk," he said sounding suddenly very serious.

239

"Why? What's going on?" I asked as the table suddenly grew quiet and attentive.

"I don't want to be a cop tonight or act like a parent, but I'm worried about you guys. I know that Jeremy has pretty much healed and is about ready to start getting adventurous again, and I want to nip something in the bud before it becomes an issue. You need to stay out of the gravel pit especially after dark. That place just isn't safe anymore."

"Why? What's the big deal?" I asked. "Moose went to Texas and is out of the picture so he isn't going to bother anyone."

"Moose's the least of your worries these days. There are some things going on at the pit that are not published and most people except for law enforcement personnel don't know about. For starters there has been some relatively major drug activity going on out there in recent months. You've heard about what's happening with the drug cartels in Mexico, well some of that crap has drifted north. We don't know if that's who's involved, but we do know that whoever it is, they are extremely dangerous and don't play games."

"Sean, you know we don't mess with that stuff," Marty protested.

"Doesn't matter! If you're in the area, you could be at risk if anything goes down out there. You don't want to find yourselves

240

in the middle of some gangland gun fight or a police sting. People get shot that way. And that isn't the only thing. Last week a high school girl was abducted and raped out there."

"From our high school?" Jamie asked. "We haven't heard anything about that. Who was it?"

"No, and you probably won't. It's being kept hush, hush until we capture the perp—if we ever do. Whether he's nabbed or not is probably irrelevant at this stage of the game. You may never hear about this one on the news because of the ages of the people involved. Their parents want to keep it as quiet as possible too. Anyway, two kids were making out in their car when some guy came up to it and asked if they would help him find his dog. He said that the dog slipped his collar to go chase a rabbit and was somewhere out in a field down the trail that runs around the lake. Naturally, they wanted to help the poor guy. He looked so crestfallen and all that.

"When they were about a quarter of a mile away, he told them that he thought his dog ran down one particular path. The threesome started down the trail, and when they were well out of sight of the main path, he pulled a gun. He made the boy put his hands behind his back where he tied him up with those cheap plastic restraints. Then he took the kid's belt and literally tied him to a tree. Then guess what happened?"

"What?" we all pretty much said in unison. In my mind, though, I kind of had an idea where this story was headed.

"At that point he aimed the gun at the girl and told her to strip. When she protested and told him that she wouldn't, he smacked her with the gun and half knocked her out. Then he proceeded to strip her himself. When he had her naked, he went up to the boy while she lay there dazed, flipped open a switch blade knife, and told him that if he made as much as a noise, he would castrate him right on the spot.

"So make sure you get the entire picture here. To start with, the girl was a virgin. That animal climbed on her and had continuous sex with her for over a half hour with her boyfriend tied to a tree watching unable to do anything to help. Every time she cried out, he hit her and told her to shut up. When he finally finished, he just pulled up his pants and walked out leaving the kids to themselves. Somehow the boy finally managed to work his way free and then helped her get dressed.

"The girl's still in the hospital. Her physical wounds are only part of the story. She may never be right mentally or emotionally again. The boy's back in school and better off by far than she is, but needs serious counseling.

"My whole point is, the gravel pit's not the same place it was a couple of years ago when it was just a teen hangout. It just isn't safe anymore. I don't want you out there especially by yourselves.

I know both of you guys think you're invincible studs, but you aren't. If you want to make out, go home and do it. Your parents are all pretty liberal. They'll let you have the den to yourselves or some other place in the house without interrupting. Hey! Jaime's dad might even let you borrow the man cave. Anyway, the point is, it's just too dangerous to be out parked someplace especially by yourselves."

With that Sean stood up, slid his chair back to where he found it, and gave us all that "look" before he took off letting us know that we should probably pay attention to what he said. We certainly didn't blow him off. The four of us talked for probably an hour about what he told us. By the time we left, we all agreed to stay out of the pit. However, for us there were more important things to worry about.

Chapter 24

Spring finally arrived and the end of the school year rapidly approached with no further signs of Bruno. Thank goodness! One evening we all went over to Jim and Sara's for late evening desert and hot chocolate. Mom Sara asked Mom if they had thought of any names yet, and that maybe she should reconsider having an ultrasound. Mom said the doctor had been applying the pressure also, but she still didn't want one. She didn't want to know the sex of the baby until he or she arrived.

She said that she knew they weren't supposed to tell if you didn't want to know, and that it was probably silly, but she just didn't want to take the chance of somebody spilling the beans and spoiling the surprise. She'd sworn the doctor to secrecy back in the beginning. She wanted no details prior to delivery except for the fact the baby appeared to be progressing normally and healthily.

I don't know what happened or why, but all of a sudden I started blubbering like an idiot. Mom asked, "Jeremy, what's wrong?"

I told them, "I don't know where that came from, but this is the hardest thing I've ever had to ask because it concerns all of us. I know you'll have to take some time to think this over, but if the baby is a boy, I really want to have his middle name be Scott. I don't care what his first name is, but that's very important to me." With that, I stood up, wiped my face with my sleeve, and said, "Ok if I go home now?"

Mom Sara stood up with me, gave me a little hug, and said, "That's fine, Jeremy, but let me fix you a little doggie bag of cookies to go."

Then I walked out, across the driveway, and into the house, and headed straight to my room. When I walked in, Scott and Mooshy sat on his bed leaning against the wall waiting for me. Both wanted the cookies so I gave the bag to them.

"Hey, Bro!" Scott said after he and Mooshy finished scarfing them down. "Thought you might need us right about now."

"I just made a big fool of myself at your mom and dad's house," I said.

Scott said, "Don't worry about it. They're over there discussing now what first names would go with Scott and other possible names in case it's a girl. Don't really know how to say it, Jeremy, but thanks. That meant a lot to me."

"You know, just between you and me, if it's a boy, I'll probably always call him little Scottie," I told him.

"Hey! It better be. One of them joked about slapping the middle name Scoterina on the baby if it's a girl. Yuck!"

***

Good Lord! Today they had Mom's baby shower. Mom Sara, Jamie, and Ashley all showed up early to do the decorations, snacks, and desserts. It turned into a perpetual hen party of giggling, plan making, decorating the nursery, naming and re-naming the kid. That brat would be so spoiled you wouldn't be able to stand him. It was getting so bad around there that Marty and I seriously considered joining a monastery.

It wasn't long after that when Dad yelled down in the family room where Marty and I had holed up playing *Mad Demons* on the computer and told us both, "Front and center!"

"Now what'd we do?" I asked Marty as we headed up the stairs.

He just shrugged his shoulders and said, "Who knows?"

When we walked into the living room, Dad, Jim Dad, and John Austin were all sitting around talking. "You two go get yourselves presentable. We're going to Detroit for a game this afternoon between the Tigers and the Yankees. You'd better wear long sleeve shirts or sweats and take your jackets. It'll get cold after the sun goes down." Jim Dad said.

"And wear belts. I don't want to see six inches of boxer shorts when we walk down the street," Dad added as Marty and I rolled our eyes at each other. I'm sure Marty and I both were thinking about the same thing—if you don't want to look at our boxers, walk in front. However, we were wise enough to keep our opinions to ourselves for a change.

"Of course, when they're hanging that low, it does make it a little more effective swatting butts if they get out of line," Mr. Austin cracked. Very funny! Marty and I thought. Ha! Ha!

The game was great! My kind of game—a regular pitcher's duel. The Tigers won 9-7. There were four home runs, lots of hits, stolen bases, and all the stuff that makes the games fun for me. The dads spent a boat load of money with hot dogs running for about five dollars a crack and soft drinks not far behind. I know Marty and I had three dogs apiece plus drinks, popcorn, and a souvenir baseball each. I'm not sure what all the dads had. Just glad Mr. Austin wasn't driving.

It was well after midnight when we finally walked into the house still stuffed to the gills, happy, excited about the game, and ready for bed. In all the time we were gone, nobody ever mentioned the baby. I don't know if the dads planned it that way or not, didn't matter. Marty and I had a ball. We quietly slipped through the door figuring Mom had gone to bed hours ago. Nope! She'd waited up for us and could hardly contain herself. You wouldn't believe all the stuff, and she had to show us everything. She also said everything would be saved including everything Sara has from Emily for when Marty and I get married and start our own families.

Suddenly Mom stopped and just looked at me for a second and then said, "Jeremy, you must have eaten way too much junk food. You look a little green around the gills. Maybe you should go to bed."

Dad could hardly keep from snorting right out loud.

Over the course of the next couple of weeks the news kind of filtered through the school as to who the kids had been at the pits that were assaulted. Both were juniors and really nice kids. The girl was quite popular and the guy was just a normal, everyday kid. He wasn't a jock of any kind and not very big. No way could he have protected the girl against her attacker even if he hadn't been tied up. The whole deal seemed pretty scary when you thought about it.

Happily the girl finally returned to school and appeared to be okay. There would be emotional scars, but, at least, physically she'd be fine. What totally blew my mind were some of the comments that supposedly were made to both the guy and the girl. Some sickos actually accused the girl of enticing the creep. Others accused the guy of getting off watching his date raped with him tied to a tree. Fortunately the assistant principal caught wind of it and cracked down on those bullying losers big time. That crap came to a screeching halt.

It was getting to be that time of the year. The prom date and place had been set and the four of us were making plans big time. The girls ordered their dresses, and Marty and I ordered our tuxes. Only one major problem remained.

"Mom, what am I going to do? I don't know how to dance!" I told her one afternoon while she was out in the kitchen getting dinner.

"What do you mean?" she asked. "You've been to dances before."

"Yeah, but I've never danced. We've always just gone and hung out on the sidelines talking while other people danced."

"Does Marty know how?" she asked.

"I doubt it. I don't think he's ever even been to one, much less danced. Bruno never let him go to anything like that. And since he's been living next door, there hasn't been a school dance."

"Well!" Mom sighed, "I guess we'll probably have to do something about it then, won't we?"

"I kind of hoped you'd say something like that."

The next thing I knew they informed Marty and me that we were invited to a command performance in our den Saturday night. That wouldn't be too embarrassing! Right! Come to find out the girls weren't all that comfortable either with their skills and needed some tutoring as well. Everyone showed up—the girls, the moms, the dads, everyone including the Austins.

"What the hell are they doing here?" I whispered to Marty.

"Probably came to make fun of us," Marty answered.

Then came the big surprise. Mr. Austin could dance very, very well. So could his wife. Never would have guessed that. They had volunteered to tutor us.

Right off the bat, he hauled Marty and me over to one corner and Mrs. Austin took the girls to the other, and our lessons began. The music that the girls provided blared as we all learned to dance. He showed us all kinds of moves and made us follow him and learn what he showed us. Actually, it didn't seem too bad. After about a half hour, we took a break.

Then they put the four of out there on the floor as well as Mr. and Mrs. Austin. We could go on our own or follow them. After another half hour, Mom cracked out the pizzas and our dancing lessons were done for the night. Now all we had to do was practice between then and the prom and we would be good to go.

The four of us had a lot of fun the next couple of weeks. We practiced whenever we could—mostly the slow dancing so we could just hold on to each other and sway back and forth and talk silliness to each other. Of course we did the fast stuff too because that's what most of it would be at the prom. However, the slow stuff was more fun. I think I was falling in love.

Chapter 25

Prom night finally came. We didn't rent a limo or anything like that. None of us had a job except for Marty and his babysitting and my part time gig at the golf course. This whole thing cost the moms and dads a bundle. Naturally, everyone wanted pictures so Marty picked up Ashley at five and then we met at Jamie's house to pick her up, have our pictures taken, and get the third degree from Mr. Austin. I think we all would have been disappointed if he hadn't.

"So, I can expect Jamie home by midnight?" he asked with his uplifted eyebrows.

"No," I responded. "The prom ends at midnight and then we go to the high school for the post-prom party. We stay there all night, have breakfast, and then they unlock the doors at eight o'clock and let us out. Nobody can leave before that. It's all part of the written agreement we signed when we plopped down our fifty dollar per couple fee."

"So tell me again about this post-prom party? It sounds like it could end up as some kind of a giant orgy or something. There are a ton of rooms in that building and they can't all be watched or supervised."

We'd gone through all of this long before when he signed the permission slip for Jamie, but he insisted on giving us a hard time by making us tell him all about it again.

"We will be confined to the gym, commons area, and the theater. They will have a security fence going across the hall way that is locked and nobody can go anywhere near the rooms," I said.

"Dad, we told you all of this before. There will be games, snacks, and all kinds of things to do through the course of the night. Also, they are going to run three different movies in the theater," Jamie told him.

"And there will be chaperones coming out of our ears," Marty piped up. "The principal and assistant principal will both be there along with the senior class sponsors and who knows who else."

"There will be some junior class parents there as well. Oh, by the way, Jamie. Don't forget to take some clothes to change into so you can get out of your formal," Ashley added.

"That's when it really gets fun," I said with a straight face. "We all get out in the middle of the commons area and strip. Last couple dressed back in their regular clothes has to run two laps around the gym in their skivvies."

"What?" Mr. Austin bellowed.

"Oh, Dad! He's pulling your leg. Now, get the pictures taken so we can get out of here, "Jamie told him.

So he did. Then just before we headed out, Mr. Austin insisted that Marty and I follow him to the den, the Man Cave. We looked at each other, rolled our eyes, and smirked. Oh, goodie! Lecture time!

When we were safely in the den with the door shut, he turned to face us. He scowled for about ten seconds and then reached into his front pocket and pulled something out. He handed both of us a fifty dollar bill. "Don't skimp on your dinners tonight, guys. This won't cover the whole bill, but it will help. Treat the girls royally like I know you will and have a great time. This is the only high-school senior prom you will ever go to so make it a really memorable experience. Now, listen! This is between us. The girls don't need to know anything about the money."

We didn't know what to say. Neither one of us thought we should take it, but he just grabbed a hold and bear hugged us both at the same time and said with a real, genuine smile on his face, "Go! You've got a whole bunch more pictures to get taken."

The girls didn't even ask. They just assumed that he dragged us back there to threaten our lives and masculinity.

From there we went back to Ashley's, then Marty's, and finally our house. Just before we walked into the house, Marty and I stopped. "Hold on a minute. We have to do something," I told the girls. Then we both reached inside of our tux trousers and grabbed our boxers and pulled them as high as we could, in effect, giving our selves wedgies. There were at least eight inches of boxer shorts showing. All four of us acted like idiots when we traipsed into the house.

Dad's eyes looked like saucers when he saw us. Mom laughed out loud, and finally he just shook his head, smiled, and said, "Okay, you got me this time. However, I am going to get a picture of both of you just like that before you straighten yourselves out."

And he did. Not only did he take pictures of Marty and me standing beside each other trying to look like complete dorks, but he also took a shot of the girls with us. Then Marty and I ran to my bedroom and put everything back in place for the real pictures. The night was off to a great start. Next stop—dinner.

We had reservations at one of the nicer restaurants. Mr. Austin's gift made it a really memorable occasion. We couldn't have afforded the shrimp appetizers and steak dinners without it. The girls never knew the difference. That's the way he wanted it, so that's the way we did it.

We arrived at the prom a little after eight all decked out in our tuxes and formals and looking like a million bucks. The band started playing before we arrived, and there were actually some couples out on the floor already dancing. We made the rounds at first greeting our friends and talking about our pre-prom experiences. Everyone had about the same story to tell—most having to do with getting in all the picture commitments and parents who worried to death about their kids.

Eventually Jamie and I wandered out on the dance floor. Our first dance was a slow one. We both kind of wanted to "warm up" with a dance that we could just kind of hold on to each other and get comfortable out there. Here I was a senior in high school and actually dancing on a real dance floor for the first time. It didn't take long to wonder why I had never done it before.

Dancing rocked! The next song sped up big time, and we stayed right out there on the floor and went after it. "Thank you, Mr. Austin!"

By our fifth or six dances, I felt really at ease and able to look around, wave at people, and relax and enjoy myself. Then, out of the blue, my heart jumped into my throat. I sensed this flash from about twenty feet across the dance floor of a kid who looked just like Scott. After the initial shock, I tried to move us over in that general direction a little bit to get a better look. However, whoever it was that I saw had vanished. At least I couldn't find him again right then. Nobody in our school even vaguely resembled him. I assumed I must have hallucinated the whole thing. Either that, or the phantom dancer was some girl's date from another school who just happened to resemble Scott.

After a couple of more dances, we decided to take a break and go get some snacks. We grabbed a table, and shortly thereafter Marty and Ashley joined us. We hadn't been there two minutes when the girls decided they had to go to bathroom together to compare notes, or whatever it is they do that always takes so much time. That was okay, though, because it gave me a minute alone with Marty.

"Marty, I had the strangest thing happen out there on the dance floor. I thought I saw Scott out of the corner of my eye. I know I had to be imagining things because I steered Jamie over in that general direction and couldn't find him."

"I wonder if he's here," Marty said. "You know, it's his senior prom too. No reason why he shouldn't be. He just might have a girl friend out there in the spirit world. Who knows what goes on with him?"

"I know, that's the scary part," I laughed. "However, you'd think he'd at least come by and say 'Hi' or something."

"You try to connect with him telepathically?"

"No, it's not an emergency. Besides, if he's here, he'll make himself known one way or the other. Oops! Time to change the subject. Here come the girls. That didn't take them nearly as long as normal."

"They just don't want us checking out their competition," I laughed.

"Hi, Jamie. Hi, Ashley. That sure didn't take long. Powder room runs are usually good for at least fifteen minutes," Marty jabbed.

"Hey," Ashley came back. "All we wanted to do was check out all the buff guys with their cute butts who are all over the place. Some of the dudes in our school cleaned up real well."

"Whoa! Not fair," I stammered feeling half embarrassed about what Marty and I had just said. "We didn't check out all the cute girls while you were gone."

"No, both of you've just been gawking at the chicks all over the place ever since we arrived without having to take a potty break to do it," Jamie said smiling.

The good natured bantering went back and forth for a couple more minutes before the band started up again with one of our favorites. They had taken a break as well. It was time to get back on the floor. We'd dance for a few songs, take breaks, come back on the floor, and just overall have a lot of fun. I had pretty much forgotten about the so-called Scott sighting.

The second set was almost over when I turned Jamie around on one of the slow, soft songs that allowed us to cling on to each other in a death grip. That's when I saw him again. Scott was dancing right beside me with some girl I'd never seen before. He looked over at me and smiled. He pointed his head at the far corner of the ballroom to an area that had been kind of roped off and told me telepathically, "You and Marty meet me over there during the next break."

I gave him an ever so slight nod of the head indicating that we would. As soon as the set ended, I grabbed Marty and let him know we were going to the john. One of the girls suggested that they wanted to go check up on some of their girl friends and see what everyone was doing. We decided to meet back at the snack area towards the end of the break.

259

Marty and I took a quick detour through the bathroom for show and then headed towards the corner of the ballroom that Scott had pointed at. When we showed up, he stood there waiting for us.

"You're here!" I said somewhat amazed. He actually looked pretty mature in a tux, nothing like the goofy Scott I knew.

"Yeah, what'd you expect? It's prom night."

"I know. I'm really glad you made it. It just really surprised me to see you," I said repeating everything Scott said so Marty would know.

"It's not just the prom for us. It's kinda like a reunion," Scott started to explain. "See all those people on the other side of the roped off area? They are all people who died while going to high school here. This year I'm the guest of honor. It's really been kind of cool. There's been speeches and everything. I even had to stand up and give a little talk to my friends. That kinda scared me, but they all applauded when I finished, so I guess I did okay."

As I looked out at all the people, I noticed that they had all dressed differently. Only a couple of the guys and girls wore formals and tuxes. Most of them had on regular clothes. Some of them seemed to be dressed really weird.

"Is your reunion like a costume party?" I asked. "Some of them look really kind of funny and out of place."

"Those who died before they started having senior proms came dressed in their regular school clothes."

"Oh, come on!" I said. "Look at that guy with the bib overalls and flannel shirt. You can't tell me he went to school dressed like that."

"Oh, that's Zeek. He died back in 1847. He and his family were building their new home across the drive from the log cabin they'd lived in since they migrated in from the New York area. He stood up in the rafters and a crow buzzed him—checking up on what he was doing I guess. He waved his hat at the crow trying to scare it away and lost his balance and fell. He died on impact. He was the first one to die from our high school."

"Now wait a minute. Our high school is only thirty years old," I protested.

"The current building is only thirty years old, but the school is over one-hundred and fifty years old. The city fathers established this town in the early 1840's. The first school started in 1845. It consisted of a one-room log school that taught kids from first through the twelfth grade. Zeek was in that first class in 1845. He'd been going to school two years when he died."

"They had the entire school district in one room? That's kind of hard to visualize," I told him.

"Zeek said there were only twenty-three kids in the whole school. His class was the biggest one and there were three people in it."

"So tell us about some of the other kids," I said. "What about that good looking hottie you're dancing with?"

"That's Maria. She died about ten years ago on prom night when a bunch of the kids took off after the dance and headed for Lake Michigan. They ran into fog on the way and some semi truck rear-ended them. Maria's the only one who died, but the other four in the car were all hurt pretty badly. The guy she dated that night turned into a human vegetable, completely mentally and physically paralyzed. She goes and visits him in the institution where they have him at least once a week. She's the only one he can communicate with. His parents and siblings used to come, but since he couldn't talk back, they figured he didn't know anything so they eventually quit coming. And that's too bad because he looked forward to and enjoyed their visits."

"That's sad. His family just abandoned him?"

"Yep! They just figured that he'd be better off dead. Anyway, that's when the post prom parties started that you're going to tonight. The idea evolved to keep kids from going out and getting themselves into all kinds of trouble after the dance."

Everyone on the other side of the roped off area had a story. Scott told us a number of them—including the old bald headed guy hanging out there with them. He'd been the principal back in the fifties. One morning while patrolling the halls outside of the gym before school started, he dropped dead of a heart attack. He was supposedly very popular with the kids and always chaperoned all the dances and events even when he didn't have to. They loved having him there because he was the one person in authority who knew all their names and stayed very approachable. Any kid could talk to him about anything anytime. Ever since he died, he's continued to chaperone all the annual reunions on prom night."

"Do they have a reunion even on years when nobody dies?" Marty asked.

"Sure do. During the rest of the year we're all out doing our own things being our normal angelic selves. On prom night we all meet."

I fake gagged on the 'angelic' comment. Anyway, it was time to get back to the girls. Hopefully, they would have all kinds of things to tell us because there wasn't much that we could tell them. We would definitely let them carry the conversation, which normally wasn't too hard to do.

The third and final set was as much fun as the first two. Jamie and I were actually getting pretty good at this dancing thing. What surprised me was how well Scott moved around out on the dance floor. He had never been on a dance floor in his life, and now that he was dead, he actually danced very well. When I asked him about it, his only comment was, "Hey! You think that all I do all day is sit around and shine my halo? You're in for a real surprise seventy or eighty years from now, Bro!

"Like you should see some of the wild parties we throw. In case you didn't notice, Zeke and some of the older ones aren't dancing. They don't know how to do this modern stuff. One night he and some of his friends put on an old fashioned barn dance."

"What's a barn dance?" I asked.

"Back in the old days when people built a house, like the one he was working on when he died, or like when someone got married, or were celebrating the end of the harvest season, they would have a big dance in someone's barn. They would mostly square dance or line dance. You know what that is?" he asked.

"Never heard of it," I said.

"Well that's where you get four couples arranged in a square, and they do a dance where some guy stands up in front of the band and calls out dance steps. You start out by bowing to your partner, and then everyone circles their arms around each other's and circle to the left and then circle to the right, and then whatever the caller calls out you do. He calls out things like dosado and promenade right or left and everyone does it. There are all kinds of wild things that they do. It's a blast. I'd never even heard of the thing either. Anyway, that's what they used to do back in Zeke's day so that's what we did."

When the prom wound to a close, the four of us headed for the car and started right out for the high school. We had to be there by twelve-thirty. The sponsors knew exactly what time the prom finished, and we had a half hour to get to the school. It only took about fifteen minutes. Trusting souls that they were had us on a damn short leash.

Chapter 26

We arrived at the post prom-party right on time. There was a regular line up at the door because the chaperones checked everyone for contraband—you know, booze, pot, and all that stuff. We were clean so they let us right in. The first thing we did was head for the john so we could get out of those stiff tuxes and formals and get into something comfortable. They had a storage room set aside where we could stash our stuff until morning. It did feel much better to be dressed normally again.

We spent the first hour talking to everyone and sharing experiences and laughs about some of the goofy things that had happened. One of the guys ordered escargot for his appetizer not having a clue what it was. When the waiter told him that he just ate snails, he ran to the bathroom and threw up much to the glee of everyone at their table. He didn't much enjoy his dinner. They said he still looked sick when they ordered dessert. I don't think his friends will ever let him live that one down.

Then someone told a really funny story about some girl who started sneezing and couldn't quit. Every time she and her date tried to dance, she started sneezing. When they left the dance floor, she'd stop. Come to find out, they discovered that she was allergic to the guy's aftershave lotion-thanks to one of the chaperones who had a similar experience one time. He'd borrowed his dad's cologne and really plastered it on. He ended up in the bathroom with his shirt and tie off washing off his face, neck, and chest so that they could continue on in peace.

I think the kids who had the most fun were the ones that went in groups, either like the four of us, or in some cases where several kids went together without specific dates. I know of one group of eight kids who went as a group with no attachments. They had a ball. Nobody had to impress a date and there was always something or someone to laugh at besides themselves.

About one o'clock some of the games kicked in. People played volleyball, badminton, and stuff like that in the gym. In the commons area there were board games, "Pro-Poker," and all kinds of stuff like that. We game hopped for a couple of hours and then decided to go in and watch the second movie in the auditorium at three. They showed a comedy, I think. All I know for sure is that the lights came on at seven and everyone in the place looked sound asleep to me. Somewhere shortly after the first half hour of the second movie, all four of us completely zonked out never to be disturbed until the lights came on. Everyone in the place looked around at each other saying, "Uh, what happened?" At that point we all started laughing at ourselves and each other.

We all felt like zombies when we wandered out of the auditorium and into the commons area where the school's cooks had starting to serve breakfast. I think almost everyone ended up asleep in the auditorium because we were some of the first ones out, and there were only a handful of people milling around. The game tables had all been cleared off and turned into breakfast tables.

After breakfast everyone left and went home. I would assume that almost everyone spent the rest of the day sacked out. At least I know I did. I crashed until two o'clock in the afternoon. From what I heard later, the rest of our group did the same thing. Scott and his date never showed up at the post prom party so I don't know what ever happened to them that night, He probably hung out with all of his reunion buddies.

After that night, life started to move on pretty normally—all we needed to do was get ourselves graduated and then we could move on with our lives.

Chapter 27

Graduation day finally came with a flurry of activity. We had to get there early in our caps and gowns and get ourselves lined up alphabetically, and, of course, receive all the orders about not doing cartwheels and embarrassing ourselves in front of our families and friends as we crossed the stage. They also suggested that we not throw our hats in the air because it'd be too hard getting our own back and that was the only thing we were allowed to keep along with our tassels. We had to turn our robes in as soon as soon as we finished. Hopefully everyone had their pictures taken in advance.

There in the front row sat an empty chair. That would have been Scott's. Our school customarily left an empty seat for any deceased class member. When I saw that empty seat, I got a huge lump in my throat knowing Scott should have been in it.

After we marched in, we had to listen to the speeches by the principal, the superintendent, the valedictorian, class president, and a guest speaker. Jamie, our valedictorian, gave her speech third. That was the only one that I really listened to even though I'd already heard it a couple of times. She'd made the three of us sit down in her living room and listen while she practiced it. Obviously, we were all horribly impressed and proud of her—even if we did have to hoot on her just a little when she rehearsed it in front of us.

After the speeches, they had the presentation of the diplomas. The president of the junior class read off the names— Amber Marie Aaronson, Loren Robert Abalone, in fond memory of Scott Andrew Adams... When she called Scott's name off, the girl behind him waited as if he actually walked across the stage. Unknown to everyone in the place except for Bobby, who sat with his mom and Sean, and me, Scott did walk across the stage and receive his diploma with Mooshy loping along at his side. For once, he actually behaved himself—no cartwheels, war whoops, or anything. That principal who died in the 1950's presented it to him and shook his hand. Then he dug in his pocket and pulled out a treat for Mooshy. His whole group of reunion friends stood around down at the base of the stage cheering and clapping for him. Scott and Mooshy left the stage and took their seats with our classmates.

After a couple more names were called came, "Jamie Rae Austin," along with a roar from the bleachers of, "That's my girl!" Several people laughed and Jamie smiled. Mr. Austin was in fine form that day. Down the line the speaker read off, "Martin Jerome Johnson, Jr." I had never heard Marty's full name before. I found out later that after his dad died in the car accident that the Jr. part was just kind of forgotten except for formal occasions.

It wasn't too much after that when they announced, "Ashley Marie Moore" to the cheers of all her family and friends. Finally they made it to the tail end of the alphabet when they finally called out, "Jeremy Wayne Wright." I had finally officially graduated and held my diploma in my hand. Scott stood below, waving his diploma in the air, while giving me a big thumbs up.

When I caught Marty alone a bit later, I had to tell him. "Marty there are a couple of things you've got to know about the ceremony today. First off, Scott walked across the stage and received his diploma when they called off his name. All of his friends from their reunion stood around beneath the stage and cheered for him as it happened. Then he even went back to his assigned seat—for a while. As soon as he took his seat, they all disappeared. That's when he turned around looking for me sporting that big fat ass grin of his.

"Now, the really big news! When you walked across the stage and received your diploma, your mom stood down there in front with Scott and cheered you on with tears in her eyes looking so

271

proud. He held her hand all the time you walked across the stage. I thought it might be your mom because she kind of looks like you, but I didn't know for sure until Scott clued me in just a few minutes ago."

The news overwhelmed Marty momentarily to learn that his mom had been there cheering for him and hadn't missed his big day. He sucked it up right away, but I knew it'd get to him later. He wanted to see her himself. He also thought it was pretty exciting that Scott had received his diploma.

After the explanations, Scott tuned onto Bobby telepathically, "Hey, little buddy. Did you see me get my diploma? Pretty neat eh? And don't forget, I'll be back here someday to watch you stroll across that stage when you get yours. I'll be standing right there in front cheering for you."

Then Scott explained to Bobby everything that had happened. He was full of curiosity. He had seen the group in front and wondered who they were. Even at his tender age, Bobby knew enough about his own special ability not to shout out at Scott when he crossed the stage. He just waited patiently until one of us explained things to him.

Sean slipped up to Marty and me, playing it cool as he shook our hands and congratulated us. Out of the corner of his mouth, he whispered, "Scott picked up his diploma today, didn't he? I want to hear all about it."

I simple nodded and said with a smile, "Isn't it about time for you to buy breakfast again?"

Life was good. Summer vacation had officially started. We had nothing to worry about until September. Right? Wrong! Very shortly all hell broke loose.

Chapter 28

It must have been two weeks after graduation when my cell phone went off. I had been sound asleep for maybe an hour and felt a little disoriented at first. At night I set my cell phone to vibrate and park it on my night stand just in case Jamie calls. Sometimes if one of us can't sleep we'll call the other.

"Hi," I said trying to sound cheerful thinking it was probably her without looking at the caller id.

"Hey! It's me. We got a problem," Marty said sounding terrified.

"What time is it?" I asked trying to clear my brain.

"One thirty or so I guess," he said. "Doesn't matter! I just received a call from Bruno and he wants us to meet him?"

"What? He called? What does he want? How'd he know you have a cell phone much less what the number is?" I asked.

"He told me that he had been keeping track of both of us in the papers during the wrestling season and had been at the state tournament. He dressed up like a maintenance man and watched us for both days. He said that he figured out which travel bag belonged to me and which one was yours. So when nobody was around he searched them both and found my cell phone. He just wrote down the number so that he would have it and put it back."

"So what does he want?"

"He wants us both to get dressed and go down to the corner and wait for him. When he's comfortable that we haven't called the police or alerted our families, he'll pick us up. He said he has something really important to discuss with us and show us out at the shed behind our old house."

"Is he nuts?" I asked a little dumbfounded. "What makes him think that we'll just slip out of the house in the middle of the night and meet him because he wants us to?"

"That's where it gets nasty," Marty replied. "He said that this will be our one and only chance to get him out of our lives forever. He said that if we meet him without telling anybody— especially that asshole cop buddy of ours, so he can clear the air with us, he'll promise to leave town and never come back. If we don't, he'll take it as a personal affront and burn down both houses in the middle of the night when people least expected it killing both families including Emily. Don't ask me how he even knew about Emily unless he saw her at the tournament."

"Doesn't sound like we have a hell of a lot of choice, does it?" I said as I started calling for Scott telepathically. "I'll meet you in front of your house in five minutes.

While I dressed, Scott and Mooshy showed up. "What's going on, Bro?" he asked. Sounds like an emergency.

"It is. Bruno just called Marty and insisted on meeting the two of us right now. He threatened both families if we called the cops or alerted anyone before leaving the house." I relayed Marty's entire conversation as I tied my Adidas.

"You're gonna call Sean before you go. That's all there is to it. Also tell him that Mooshy and I are going to ride along and do whatever it takes to protect you. I don't like the sounds of this one bit."

"Let's just hope that he's telling the truth and really just wants to clear the air before he leaves town."

"Bull! Call Sean now!" Scott demanded as I pulled out my phone and hit the speed dial.

"What?" he asked when he answered, not sounding particularly happy to hear from me in the middle of the night. Can't imagine why!

I told him what Marty had said hoping he would have a suggestion or two. I also let him know that Scott had showed up and planned to go with us in Bruno's truck to the shed.

"Play along with him. I'll have the place covered before you get there. In the meantime, when you walk out of the house, call me back and leave your phone turned on in your pocket so we can track it if we need to. When you get to the shed, just keep talking. I don't trust him one bit. Whatever you do, don't agitate him on purpose. Talk to him very softly and pretend to cooperate with him all the way." And then he clicked the end button on his cell phone.

When I walked outside, I hit redial and slipped the phone into my pocket. Marty sat on the stoop to his front door waiting for me. I cut across the driveways and met him as he stood up.

"I don't like this one bit," Marty said. "I don't trust that fat bastard any farther than I can throw him."

"I called Sean and Scott," I told him "Sean told me to call him again when I left the house and put it in my pocket. I did that already. Anyway, he said to cooperate with whatever Bruno says and to talk real softly to him and try to stay low key. He said he'd

277

get to the shed before we do and not to worry. He doesn't want us to get the jerk all angry or excited before we get out there. Who knows what that nut case might do if he lost it in route! Scott and Mooshy are with us and will do whatever's needed in case things go bad."

"Thank God! Hi, Scott! At least people will know what happened to us."

"Don't talk that way," Scott told him. "Everything's gonna to be fine. Now, where are we supposed to meet him?"

"He said to wait here on the corner. When he's convinced there're no cops around, he'll pick us up."

When the four of us got to the corner, we kinda stood around like a bunch of teenage hoods and waited. Scott remained the calmest of the group and kept talking to us letting us know that everything would be okay.

Shortly before Bruno showed up, I panicked. "I don't know how much battery life I have left on my cell. I haven't charged it lately. It'll probably die before we get to wherever it is we are actually going."

Scott growled at me, "I told you not to worry. I've already taken care of it. I charged your battery as well as Sean's. No energy will run out of either one of them tonight even while they're turned on and running. For cripes sake, don't sweat the petty crap! Just concentrate on keeping your cool. Now start smiling and pretend like you're happy to see him. Bruno's in that pickup coming down the street right now."

When Bruno pulled to a stop beside us, Marty opened the door and jumped in with me right behind him. "Hi, Bruno," Marty said all cheerful like. "Good to see you. It's been a really long time."

"Hi Bruno," I said. "How's it going? I hear you have something really cool to show us out at the shed."

"Yeah, I do," Bruno said. "However, it is so cool that I can't take a chance on anyone trying to pocket any of it so I want both of you to turn around in your seat and put your hands behind your backs so I can slip on these little plastic doo-dads. They'll be real easy for you to get out of once we leave the shed."

"Uh, you're gonna tie us up?" I asked.

"Shut up and do it," Scott yelled at me.

"Yeah, now turn around," Bruno said all kind of confused that we would even question it.

I nudged Marty in the ribs to get his attention, "Sure thing, Bruno. Some little voice in my ear says that it's probably a good

279

idea. That way you don't have to worry about protecting your little surprise."

So we both turned out backs to him and let him tie us up with some cheap plastic wrist restraints. Then he took off and headed for the outskirts of town where their old deserted home stood. I could breathe a little more easily knowing that at least we were headed in that direction and not someplace totally different where we would have to rely on Sean tracking us. Not a whole lot of talking went on which was okay too. As we started to get close, I looked all over the place for some sign of the police presence that Sean had promised would be there. I didn't see a thing and Scott didn't say anything. He and Mooshy sat in the back storage area behind the seats. The trip to the house only about took ten minutes, but there were times when I sensed that they'd disappeared. Then, I'd realize that they'd returned. I didn't know what they were doing.

When we pulled into the circular drive that ran around the house, he drove straight back to the shed and stopped right in front of the door. Bruno crawled out and walked around the car and opened the passenger door to let us out.

"Okay, boys. Come with me," he ordered as we clumsily swung around in the seat and managed to get out of the truck without falling flat on our faces. Never realized how much I use my hands for balance.

When we walked inside the shed, the first thing I saw was this huge, oversized barrel parked on something that looked like a small forklift and a couple of old beat up folding chairs positioned behind it. On the floor beside the barrel lay a huge dead opossum that looked like road kill.

"Have a seat, boys while I tell you a little story," Bruno said.

Like what other choice did we have? We sat down and he immediately grabbed a rope off the shelf and tied us to the chairs including our legs so we couldn't just stand up and run. Then he started to talk.

"Marty, you've been a dam pest ever since your mom dragged you along when we first got hitched. I wanted her to leave you with her relatives, but she wouldn't hear of it. She thought we could all be one big happy family. Ha! Fat chance of that! And Jeremy, you've been a royal pain in the ass since day one too. So now, I'm finally going to get my due.

"So far everything I've tried has flopped. It's been one piece of bad luck after another. Marty, when you first started driving, I discovered that you were driving that lady's car that's been babysitting you. It's disgusting the way those people took you in just like you were theirs and actually like you. That's a crock of bull. You should be living in a damn cardboard box under a bridge someplace. Anyway, thinking that you'd be driving the car, I rigged the brakes so they'd slowly lose fluid and that you'd be out racing around like the typical stupid teenager you are and end up killing yourself. So what happens? The fluid drained out too fast and that broad ran into a telephone pole backing out of the driveway. How unlucky was that!"

"I figured my next brain storm would work out even better, but it ended up as an even greater disappointment. Jeremy, I've been watching your family too and knew your old man opened up that architectural firm every morning where he works. When I loosened the gas pipe that Friday evening, I figured it would have the entire weekend to load up with gas. The explosion should've been big enough to not only wipe him off the face of the earth, but everyone and everything within blocks of the place. I had such great plans! After he was dead, I intended to rig up a bomb for the funeral home where I could wipe out what was left of both of your worthless families during the service. That turned into another piece of bad luck."

"But, why?" I asked softly trying to keep Sean's instructions in mind. "Why did you want to kill innocent people? None of our parents have ever done anything to you. They've never even seen you."

"Innocent nothing! They're both of your families now so they deserve to die too. The world will be a better place without any of you. So later tonight after you are both dead and disposed of, I'm going to burn down both of your houses and kill all of them."

"But, but... you promised!" Marty said in little above a whisper.

"I lied!" Bruno said laughing out loud. "Now, watch this."

With that he picked up the opossum that he had thrown on the floor beside the barrel and tossed it in. The liquid in the barrel bubbled and smoked for a few seconds and then quit. It was full of some kind of acid. We watched in horror with wide open eyes and mouths while it happened. It didn't take a Rhodes Scholar to figure out what he had planned for us.

After the barrel quit gurgling, Bruno turned back to us. "The lucky one dies first. We'll determine that later by lottery. The way I planned it, the unlucky one gets to watch me slit the throat of his buddy and dump his worthless dead carcass into the barrel. I figure I should only do one of you at a time. If the barrel was bigger, I could do both of you together. Wouldn't that be just clubby as hell? Anyway, after you're both dead and dissolved, I'll take the barrel out behind the shed where I already dug a big hole with that backhoe. You, the barrel, and the acid will all end up in the hole and buried tonight before I go and wipe out your families. Pretty neat plan, don't you think? After that, I'll get a good night's sleep in my old bed inside the house, and then casually drive out of town tomorrow morning just like I promised—never to return."

"I think you're one sick bastard!" Marty said glaring at him.

283

"Congratulations!" Bruno chirped. "You've won the lottery. You get to die second after watching what happens to that useless piece of crap sitting beside you."

Oh, no. Marty had done just exactly what Sean had warned us against. Where's Scott? Where's Mooshy? Where's Sean? Where're the rest of the cops?

Bruno slowly meandered over to the work bench and picked up a large butcher knife and started this weird laughter under his breath and then started singing this song I had never heard before. It terrified me. He actually planned to cut our throats and throw us in that barrel of acid.

"Freeze!" came a loud shout at the shed's double doors as they flew open with Sean's pistol drawn and aimed directly at Bruno. "Drop the knife and step out here with your hands up."

Standing beside Sean were Scott and Mooshy looking more natural than they ever have since they died. They didn't look the least bit shadowy to me.

"Freeze your ass!" Bruno yelled at him. "There ain't no way you're stopping me this time. Instead of two worthless turds in the barrel, now we're gonna have four plus that mangy looking cur!" Apparently Bruno saw them too.

Instantly he raised the knife over his head and started right at Sean. And then it happened. A deafening roar erupted as the eighty-five pound Mooshy charged him with his jaws wide open. Bruno stopped dead in his tracks just before Mooshy's jaws clamped down on his crotch. He screamed at the top of his lungs, did a three hundred and sixty degree pirouette, tripped over a 12x12 inch block of wood on the floor, and dove head first into that huge barrel of acid.

The last thing out of his mouth was, "Noooooooo!"

Marty and I reflexively reefed our chairs backwards tipping over in the process avoiding any splash over of the acid.

Lying on the floor, we watched. At first his feet flailed wildly as they stuck out of the top of the steaming, bubbly, stinking barrel of acid, and then they slowly disappeared down into the vat. I puked all over myself. So did Marty. We were a mess. Then the place filled with cops as Sean stooped down and cut us loose. He helped us both to our feet. I looked around and Scott and Mooshy had disappeared again.

"Boy! Am I ever glad he tripped over that big hunk of wood so that I didn't have to shoot him," Sean said loud enough that several of the other officers who had just shown up on the scene heard. Obviously, that would be all of our statements du jour at the investigation that had to come later. Bruno charged Sean, tripped over the wood block, and fell head first into the barrel. End of story.

They hustled us out of the shed and into the house to clean us up best they could and settle us down. They talked some about taking us to the emergency room to check us over, but neither one of us wanted to do that. We just wanted to go home.

There were a few seconds there when Marty and I found ourselves alone. "I saw both Scott and Mooshy," he whispered to me.

"I know. I'm pretty sure both Sean and Bruno did too. We'll have to check that out later.

Mom, Dad, Jim, and Sara all showed up at the scene shortly thereafter. Jamie had raced over after a frantic phone call to the Austin's and was staying with Emily—Ashley was out of town and not available.

The four moms and dads hugged us both even if we looked completely gross and stunk like a bucket of vomit. Nobody really seemed to care. Later Sean sat the six of us down at the kitchen table at Marty's old house and re-hashed the evening's events so that everyone would have all the details at the same time including Bruno's attempts on everyone's lives and his intentions for later that evening.

When he finished, and everyone had all their questions answered, Marty suddenly turned real serious and faced Sara and Jim with tears in his eyes. "I'm to blame for all of this. If it hadn't been for me, none of your lives would have been threatened or in danger. I think it would probably be best if I just packed up and left tonight when we get home. You've got to hate me for everything that's happened."

Jim looked at him and smiled, "Marty, the only place you're going when we get home is into the shower and then to bed. Besides, you have to be up in time to make it over to Ginny's house by noon to babysit Bobby. We forgot to tell you that she called earlier."

"I'm afraid you're stuck with us, Sweetheart," Sara told him as she hugged him again. "It just so happens we do love you." Then she reached over, took his chin, and turned his head so he was looking her right in the eye. "Besides, if you think for one minute that I'm going to try to explain to Emily why her Marty isn't at home, you've got another think coming, young man!"

That pretty much broke the tension as we all laughed, stood up, and headed for home, shower, and bed.

I caught Sean alone for just a minute as we were ready to leave, "What'd you see?" I asked.

"Everything," he said. "Why else wouldn't I have just shot him when he started towards me? When Mooshy charged, he ran right in the line of fire. I couldn't shoot for fear I'd hit him. Silly, isn't it. He's already dead, but I didn't even think of that at the time. All I know is that it all ended perfectly when those huge jaws grabbed him in the crotch causing that head first dive into the acid. Touché!"

It must have been almost sunrise by the time I made it home. If you can believe it, Jamie wouldn't even give me a hug or kiss! Laughing, I headed for the upstairs, showered the vomit and smell off of me, and crawled into bed. That's when I said, "Thanks, Scottie. Thanks, Mooshy. I owe both of you big time. I don't know how I'll ever repay you. I..."

"Yeah, yeah! Okay, can it! Now would you please shut the hell up? We're trying to get some sleep over here."

Sure enough, they were both in the bed across the room where they always slept. I didn't care what he said about my disturbing them; I crawled out of bed, went over and gave them both a hug. Scott smiled and told me to beat it, and Mooshy gave me a couple of big laps across the face with his stubby tail thumping the bed big time.

I knew I wouldn't be able to sleep when I crawled back into bed. I was too wired. However, I think I woke myself up for a second or two when my head hit the pillow. I'd gone out like a light. In the morning I checked my phone to see if I had any text messages from Jamie. The battery was dead.

I've attended four funerals in my life and each one has been completely different. The first one was my grandma's. She was old and had been sick for a long time, and everyone said it was a blessing when she died. Then I had to go to Scott's funeral. Scott died at sixteen, and that had to be the most horrible, traumatic experience I've ever suffered through in my life. After that I went to Marty's mom's funeral. I'd never met her so I went solely to support Marty in his pain. All of my emotions during that service were aimed right at him, not his mom. There would be no funeral service of any kind for Bruno. The local authorities came to their house and gave Marty his options. He was firm. Not only did he not want a service, but he didn't even want to know where they buried him—if there was anything left to bury. He didn't care. I wonder if he'll ever change his mind.

The time had come for our lives to continue as normally as possible. Nothing left to do before college begins in the fall except to enjoy the summer and get my little brother or sister born. Should be pretty uneventful. However…

The End

Coming Soon

Taming Young Ike

By
Larry Webb

Chapter 1

Andy grunted as he tried to hoist the root ball of the flowering crabapple tree over the mound of dirt and into the freshly dug hole. Jen stood beside him with a grin on her face holding the shovel.

"Come on, Andy, heave! Show some muscle. Do I have to show you how this is done?"

"Aaargh!" Andy screamed as he dragged the damned tree over the pile of dirt and let it slide down into the hole. "There, that's done! Now you get the easy part, filling in the hole. Hop to it, Jenny."

Laughing and picking on each other, they hadn't even noticed the mail truck that had stopped by the box at the curb. The driver had climbed out of the cab and started waddling towards them. In fact, he'd made it up to within about ten feet when they first noticed him. He waved a letter at them and called out, "Got a registered letter for Mr. Andrew John Stevens at this address. That you?"

"Yeah, that's me," Andy answered.

"Ok, sign here," he said. He handed Andy the little electronic device where he had to scrawl his name.

Andy signed in the appropriate space and handed the letter to Jenny as he grabbed the spade to fill in the hole. They watched for a minute as the postman headed back to his truck. A twelve-inch swath of sweat ran from his collar to the bottom of his butt.

"This ninety degree heat today must be a little tough on a five-foot, eight-inch, three hundred pounder," Andy commented. "Bet those leather seats are hot. He smelled pretty ripe too."

"Who's Mandy?" Jen asked.

"I don't know. Why?"

"You just signed for a letter from Mandy with no return address that's post marked from Florida."

"Well, open it up and see what it is. I didn't even look. Figured it had something to do with the wedding."

"It's addressed to you. You open it," Jenny insisted handing the letter back to him.

Andy, who had worked up a pretty good sweat on his own planting the tree, wiped his hands off on his pants, used his shirt to wipe his dripping face, took the letter from Jenny, and ripped it open.

The first thing he spied was a four by six inch glossy print. All of a sudden, his body felt like it had been hosed down by a fire truck. Sweat gushed out of his pores, and he started shaking. Staring back at him from that damned photo was an almost perfect miniature clone of himself. "Oh, shit!" he said. "This can't be!"

"What is it, honey? You look like you're having some kind of panic attack. Is something really wrong?"

He yanked the typed note out of the envelope and read it.

"Dear Andy,

Isaac Andrew Stevens (AKA Ike) turned nine in February. I realize that you've never known anything about him, and I always intended to keep it that way. However, due to circumstances beyond my control, it became clear that Ike needed to meet his father. His plane will arrive at Capitol City International Airport Saturday morning at 9:45 on flight 1620 from Miami for a two-day visit and a chance to meet and get to know you. Hope this doesn't catch you at a bad time.

Love, Mandy.

PS—FYI, Ike's a little peeler."

Andy's head started spinning. Jen could tell he was in trouble and grabbed his arm. She led him over to the steps by the front door of the house and turned him around.

"Sit down before you fall in a heap and let me see that," she told him as she snatched the mail out of his hands.

Jen scanned the letter and looked at the picture. Totally out of character for her, she absolutely freaked out spewing vulgar and profane language that Andy had never heard her use before. If nothing else, Jen always acted and talked like a lady. After her initial outburst, she calmed down enough to at least sound a little more rational—kind of, "Oh, no! No way in hell! We aren't meeting that plane. There's no way I'm becoming a step-mother to some nine year old brat two weeks before my wedding, even if it is for just two days. I don't have time for this! I'll shoot the freaking plane down first! Call her up and tell her no way—maybe later in the summer—maybe next summer—maybe never, but not now! Hell, no!"

"But, Jen! God, he is kinda cute! Look at him! He looks just like I did when I was a little kid. I can't deny him." Andy laughed, embarrassed and babbling—not really knowing what to say. He had a kid, and he liked the looks of him in the picture anyway—peeler or not. This could be fun.

"No way in hell! Not gonna happen!"

"Oh, come on! She said it was only for a couple of days, and I have no way of getting in touch with her anyway. She didn't leave a phone number or address. Besides, what can it hurt? We'll entertain him Saturday and Sunday and put him back on the plane Monday or whenever his return ticket says, and off he'll go. We'll be rid of him, and then we can go on about our own business of getting ready for the wedding. Besides, you're just jealous 'cause his Florida tan will be darker than the one you've been working on."

"Andy, what's the biggest surprise here, learning that you've got a kid out there or having this perfectly timed visit?" she asked sarcastically. "Or is this whole thing an Oscar winning charade on your part? Any chance of any more little Ikes running around out there that you supposedly don't know anything about?"

"Absolutely not!" he said emphatically, hoping like hell he was telling the truth.

"We've got to finish planting that damned tree and water it before it dies on us," Jennie snarled at him. "Maybe while we're at it you'd like to tell me a little of the background regarding young Mr. Ike? I think I do have a right to know."

Feeling nauseous, Andy walked back over to the hole where he had plopped the tree that they had bought to commemorate their brand new home, marriage, and life together. And here he'd thought the damned mailman was dragging in more RSVPs for the reception. Ordering more prime rib would have been a snap compared to this.

Struggling to remember back ten years for the details, he related the story the best he could. "Mandy's the girl I took to the senior prom in high school. Remember, now, we were only eighteen," he told her. "Anyway, our post-prom party ended up with the two of us hidden behind some trees at the very back of the golf course parking lot chugalugging a twelve pack of beer. Sometime during the middle of the night or early morning I woke up all alone in the back seat of my dad's car with my pants down around my ankles and some damn cop banging on the window with his flashlight. Fortunately, all he did was tell me to get dressed and then get my ass home—after he checked to see if I had sobered up enough to drive yet. Nothing humiliating about that, huh! He even made me pick up all the empty cans we'd tossed out the window. I never saw her again so I never found out when Mandy left or where she went."

"Yeah, that sounds real classy," Jen remarked keeping a straight face. "And here I thought all this time I'd snagged myself a virgin."

"Yeah, right! I just wonder how she got our address? We've only been here a week, for Christ's sake. Somehow real estate sales and property information like this has to be out there someplace on the Internet."

"Either that or somehow she still knows someone here in town who's been keeping tabs on you all these years for her. Joy, joy! Just what the hell we need, somebody spying on us for your old girlfriend. Hard to believe this happening just two weeks before the big day is a coincidence.

The next day and a half raced by. There were so many preparations left for the wedding. Everything had to be perfect. Period! They'd worked too hard and too long for it to be anything else.

Andy couldn't get his mind off of young Ike. What would they do with a nine year old for a couple of days? He hoped the kid wouldn't mind sleeping on the couch. The guest room sat completely empty except for a few boxes of stuff they hadn't unpacked yet.

Unfortunately, Jenny's reaction to the Ike situation didn't do a lot for their relationship. Every time Andy mentioned Ike's name or made a suggestion about how they'd entertain him for the weekend, she screamed at him, "I don't have time for this!" and stormed out of the room. After trying a few times to discuss it, Andy finally gave up and figured that the least said about the impending visit, the better. They had too many other little details left to take care of.

So, other than the outbursts when Andy mentioned Ike, and with the help of a little Xanax and a few beers, they managed to survive the next two days without any more full-fledged temper tantrums, major fights, or even any threats of cancelling the wedding. Time flew!

Made in the USA
Charleston, SC
25 June 2011